# PROTECTOR PANTHER

# PROTECTOR PANTHER

## PROTECTION, INC.
## # 3

ZOE CHANT

# AUTHOR'S NOTE

This book stands alone. However, it's the third in a series about Protection, Inc., an all-shifter private security agency. If you'd like to read the series in order, the first book is *Bodyguard Bear*, the second is *Defender Dragon*, and the fourth is *Warrior Wolf.*

# TABLE OF CONTENTS

# CHAPTER ONE

## *Catalina*

Catalina Mendez strolled down the empty street at 3:00 AM, humming to herself.

It was her favorite time of day— night— well, technically morning, even though it was dark as night. Statistically speaking, a high percentage of bad things happened at 3:00 AM. It was a peak time for vehicle crashes, industrial accidents, medical crises, and violent crimes. For an adrenaline junkie paramedic on the late shift, it was the best and most exciting time to work, when she might actually get to save a life. It didn't hurt that Catalina was a night owl, working at peak efficiency by night and a little sleepy and slow by day.

But right now, she wasn't just at peak efficiency. She was *wired.* She'd just flown back from the small European country of Loredana, where she'd been working with Paramedics Without Borders to help restore emergency services after a catastrophic earthquake.

Her return trip had been a catastrophe all by itself. Her best friend and paramedic partner Ellie McNeil had been supposed to pick her up at the airport, but her flight had been delayed, then canceled, then restored so many times that Catalina had finally texted Ellie to forget about it. Catalina was perfectly capable of taking a taxi whenever the hell her flight got in. Which had been originally scheduled for 6:00 PM on Wednesday, but turned out to be 2:00 AM on Friday.

By the time the plane took off, she'd drunk several gallons of coffee to make sure she didn't doze off in the airport and miss her flight. Then she figured she might as well drink some more, since she was already wide awake. By the time the plane touched down in Santa Martina, she'd worked up a pretty good caffeine rush. Her nerves tingled with anticipation that something exciting and important might happen at any second.

That was when she discovered that her luggage had been accidentally routed to Singapore. Which was certainly exciting and important, but not in a good way. She picked up her purse, which was all she'd taken on the plane, and made her way to the taxi stand.

As the taxi headed toward her home, she realized how little she wanted to go there. It would be boring. And lonely. She couldn't even reunite with her cats— Ellie had taken them while Catalina was away. Her bed would be cold and empty without any kitties to cuddle.

Thoughts of Ellie and bed led to thoughts of the man who now shared Ellie's bed, hot bodyguard Hal Brennan. And the other hot bodyguards at Hal's private security company, Protection, Inc. Ellie had promised to introduce Catalina to them when she got back from Loredana. She'd even offered to send photos, but though Catalina had been impressed with the pics of Hal, she'd declined to look at the ones of the single guys. She'd meet them in person eventually, and she liked being surprised.

The taxi stopped at a red light. Catalina recognized the silhouette of a towering office building a couple blocks ahead. It had been in one of the photos Ellie had emailed her, of her and Hal standing in front of Protection, Inc.

"Let me off here," Catalina said impulsively. "It's walking distance from my home."

The taxi driver craned his head at her. "Are you sure? It's a pretty long walk. And it's the middle of the night."

"I'm sure," she said.

Catalina paid him and stepped out on to the empty street. Sure, no one would be at Protection, Inc. But she'd at least get a closer look at the place she'd heard so much about. And she needed to burn off some energy before she went home, or she'd never get to sleep. Besides, night was the best time to walk around the city. The air was cool, the sky was a pretty purple-orange with light spill, and you never knew what might happen.

A vision of her mother popped into her mind as she walked down the street.

*Walking alone at night in the city!* Mom's remembered voice was loud in her ears. *You could be robbed! You could be murdered! You could* witness *a murder, like your poor friend Ellie! Why are you always so reckless?*

*It's a good neighborhood, mom,* Catalina replied to the voice in her head, echoing real conversations they'd had a thousand times over. *I'm not reckless. I'm just not afraid.*

*You should be,* Mom scolded. *Ever since you were a little girl, you haven't known the meaning of fear. I pray every night that when you do find out, it won't be too late.*

The street was empty and silent. As Catalina came closer to the towering office building that housed Protection, Inc., she saw that she was approaching a dark alley.

Normally she would have walked right past it. What were the odds that a mugger was lurking at a deserted street on the unlikely chance that someone would walk straight past his lurking area— especially when every woman Catalina had ever met, even her brave friend Ellie, would cross the street to avoid that alley?

But tonight Catalina hesitated. An odd feeling made her stomach clench and her palms tingle.

*Oh, no,* she thought, dismayed. *I spent months living in a tent in a disaster zone, and* now *I get sick?*

Then she recognized the sensation. It wasn't one she felt often, but she knew what it was. It was fear.

She stopped to take stock, wondering what had made her feel afraid. Some little thing in the environment, too subtle for her to register consciously, must have signaled that something was wrong. Something was dangerous.

Catalina took a step to the side, meaning to cross the street. She wasn't *completely* reckless. If an action seemed both dangerous and pointless, she wouldn't take it.

A man staggered out of the alley, fetched up hard against the wall of the nearest building, and slid down to the ground.

Catalina ran to him. On her way, she took a quick peek into the alley to make sure the scene was safe before she entered it. That was the part of the paramedic test she'd almost flunked, but it was second nature now. She couldn't see all the way into the alley, but what she did see was empty and still, with nothing stirring but a few discarded candy wrappers. There was no obvious danger, no pursuing muggers or smoke or sparking electrical wires, so she was free to tend to her patient.

*See?* She told the mom-in-her-head. *Not reckless!*

Catalina knelt by the man's side, giving his body a quick visual scan before she did a more detailed examination. His eyes were closed. He was tall and muscular, but lean rather than bulky. His short black hair looked soft as a cat's fur. He wore dark jeans and a white T-shirt spotted with fresh blood. More blood ran down his handsome face from a cut at his temple. His chest was moving evenly, and when she bent over him, she couldn't hear any sounds that indicated breathing difficulties. His skin seemed pale, but it was difficult to tell in the hard white glare of the street lights.

Airway: good. Breathing: good. Visible bleeding: not severe. He wasn't likely to drop dead in the next few seconds, so she'd call 911 to get the ambulance on its way before she resumed her assessment.

She opened her purse and pulled out her cell phone, then stared at it in dismay. It was her phone from Loredana, which wouldn't work in the US. She must have accidentally packed her regular phone in her suitcase. Which was in Singapore.

"Dammit!"

Her patient woke as if she'd fired a gun in the air. His body jerked, he sucked in a sudden breath, and his eyes flew open. They were blue as ice, and they fixed on her with an unsettling intensity.

"Who are you?" he demanded.

*Level of consciousness: alert and responsive*, Catalina thought.

She spoke in the soothing tones she always used on trauma victims. "I'm a paramedic. Is it all right if I help you?"

Legally, she had to ask permission before she did anything to anyone. Almost all of her patients automatically said yes.

The man patted his hip, then his shoulder. His eyes narrowed in a quick flicker of dismay. "I've lost my weapons. And I can't—" He broke off, looking frustrated. "I can't protect you. So no. I don't give you permission to treat me. Get out of here."

He struggled to get up, but only managed to get as far as propping himself on his elbows. More blood ran down his face. He clearly wasn't going anywhere.

"Why don't you lie back down?" Catalina suggested, turning up the soothing. "Just let me take a look at you."

"No." Most men raised their voices when they were angry or upset, but this man lowered his. It was more forceful than if he'd yelled.

"I'm a paramedic," Catalina repeated. Sometimes trauma victims were too shocked or disoriented to take in what she said the first time. "I can help you. Can you tell me what happened?"

He might be a trauma victim, but he wasn't disoriented. Those ice-blue eyes of his seemed to look right through her, as if he knew things about her that even she didn't. "If you're a paramedic, then you need my consent before you treat me. I'm not giving it. Take your phone and go. Once you're in a safe place, call—"

"That phone doesn't work in America," she interrupted him.

The man let out an exasperated breath. He again tried to get up, and again failed.

"Why can't you stand up?" Catalina asked. "Are you dizzy? Or is something wrong with your legs?"

"Both," he muttered, sounding reluctant to admit it. "I've been drugged. They ambushed me with a tranquilizer rifle."

"With a *tranquilizer rifle?*"

She'd once treated a woman who'd been the victim of friendly fire from zookeepers trying to take down an escaped capybara. Catalina had never heard of a capybara before, but it turned out to be a guinea pig the size of a sheep. It had been one of her all-time favorite calls. But that tranquilizer dart hadn't caused dizziness and paralysis, it had immediately knocked the woman unconscious. And who would use one for an ambush? Criminal… veterinarians?

Then Catalina realized the important part of what he'd let slip. "If you've been drugged, it's the same as if you were unconscious. I can assume that you *would* consent to treatment if you were in your right mind. So settle down. I just want to check you for life-threatening injuries."

His eyebrows rose in disbelief, as if it was the first time in his life that anyone had the nerve to stand up to him. Then he took a deep breath, seeming to concentrate.

Her stomach clenched. Her palms tingled. Her heart began to pound.

Nothing about the man had changed, but she suddenly knew he was dangerous. Very dangerous. Lethal. She had to run— she had to save herself—

The phone fell from her hand, the screen shattering. She scrambled to her feet, stumbling backward, desperate to get away.

*But he hasn't threatened me,* she thought. *He hasn't attacked me.*

He was still sprawled on the ground, bleeding, his gaze locked on hers. Deadly. Terrifying.

*He's injured. He can't walk. He needs help.*

All her instincts screamed at her to run. She was gasping, her pulse thundering in her ears, sweat pouring down her face and back. She'd never been so scared in her entire life.

*Never abandon a patient.*

It was the hardest thing she'd ever done, but Catalina took a step forward. Then another step. Then she dropped back down on her knees beside him.

Her terror vanished as if it had been switched off like a light. The man rested his head on his arms, exhaustion etching lines around his strong features.

"I don't believe this," he muttered. "I hit you with both barrels. I laid it on so hard, I wore myself out! How are you still here?"

She stared at him. "You did that on purpose? How?"

"Practice." He raised his head. His intense gaze again fixed on her, but now she felt no fear. He had beautiful eyes. They were an astonishingly clear blue, like an early morning sky, fringed with thick black lashes.

"I've got some very bad people after me. You could get caught in the crossfire if you stay with me. But since you were playing hooky when God gave out fear…" As if against his will, he gave her an ironic smile. It transformed the hard angles of his face, making her notice again how good-looking he was. "If you can help me get up and walk a block, I can get us both into a secure building. Once we're inside, we'll be safe. I have friends I can call."

As an afterthought, he added, "I'll give you permission to examine me then. I know you're dying to check me out."

She couldn't tell if he was making a double entendre or a statement of fact. Strange guy. Strange hot guy who'd been ambushed with a tranquilizer rifle and could terrify you just by looking you in the eyes. Strange brave guy who preferred sacrificing himself to putting a stranger at risk.

Catalina crouched low. "Put your arm around my shoulders."

"I know the drill." He propped himself up on his left arm and put his right arm around her shoulders. It was warm, not cold with shock. Having his arm around her made her feel oddly safe and secure. As if he was protecting her, though he couldn't even walk.

She gripped his right wrist, unable to help noticing that he had amazing biceps. Amazing arms in general. Even his wrist was thick with muscle. Strange, totally ripped guy.

Strange sexy guy who knew unusual things. He knew how to do an assisted walk, and he knew the laws of consent for treatment.

"Are you a paramedic?" she asked, wrapping her left arm around his waist. He was warm all over.

He shook his head, struggling to get his legs under him. "I mean, yes, I am. But that's just a qualification, not my job. I'm— I *was*— a PJ. That's—"

"Air Force pararescue. Special Ops combat search and rescue," Catalina filled in. Quoting a poster she'd seen, she added, "Because sometimes even Navy SEALs have to call 911."

"That's right." His breath came harsh in her ear. He couldn't seem to move his legs at all, though she could feel his attempts through the tensing and flexing of his other muscles against her body. But though he'd said bad guys could descend on them at any second, his voice and expression remained calm. "Did you ever want to be one?"

"Yeah, but they don't take women." Then she stared at him. "How'd you know?"

"You've got the right stuff. Mentally, I mean." Then he let out a frustrated breath and stopped struggling to move. "I hope you've got the right stuff physically, too, because we can't do an assisted walk. My legs are completely paralyzed. You'll have to drag me. Or I could give you the code to the building. It's only a block away. You could go in and call for help—"

"Forget it," she replied. "I'm not leaving you."

He smiled, but not the same amused, catlike smile she'd seen before. This one held infinite depths of sadness and regret over its pleasant surface. "Never leave a fallen comrade, huh? Are you an airman? A Marine?"

"No, I've never served," Catalina replied. "And I'd rather not drag you. I don't know what kind of injuries you have. Do you know?"

"I'm not sure," he admitted. "The tranquilizer knocked me for a loop. I don't remember the fight too well. I'm not even sure exactly how I got here."

She glanced at the blood on his shirt. If he had internal injuries, she definitely shouldn't drag him. "I'll do a fireman's carry."

He gave her a doubtful glance, which didn't surprise her. He had to be over a foot taller and fifty pounds heavier than her. Then he shrugged. "Okay. Let's give it a try."

Catalina wrestled him over her shoulders, thanking her lucky stars that she'd just spent months in a disaster zone without any high-tech amenities. If it hadn't built up her strength moving heavy equipment and patients, she probably couldn't even have gotten him into position.

She stood up, careful to lift from her legs, not her back. He weighed even more than she'd imagined. Her knees cracked audibly, and she staggered.

"Easy." He laid a steadying hand on her forearm. "Find your center of gravity and settle into it."

"Thanks," she gasped, regaining her balance. "Which way?"

"Forward. I'll tell you when we get there."

She took a step forward, trying not to pitch forward under his weight. Her breath burned in her lungs, and her back and legs and neck ached. She didn't feel like she could make it five more steps, let alone an entire city block. But her other choice was dragging him over the sidewalk and maybe making his injuries worse. She took another step, and then another one.

Another step. Another.

A quarter of a block.

Her face felt hot and swollen with blood. Her back was on fire.

Another step. Another.

Half a block. Catalina felt like she was about to pass out. She could see nothing but a red haze.

"You're strong," he said quietly.

Hearing that from a PJ— hearing it from this man, in particular—

gave her strength.

Another step.

He suddenly whipped his arm out like he was slapping something out of the air. The shift in weight nearly knocked her off her feet. As she staggered, trying to regain her balance, she saw some tiny object rolling across the sidewalk.

"Put me down and run!" he said sharply.

"No!" A pain like a needle jab pricked her arm. "Ow!"

Everything spun around her, and she hit the ground hard. Catalina couldn't so much as twitch. When she tried to speak, she found that not even her lips would move. But now she was close enough to the ground to see the tiny object on the sidewalk: a tranquilizer dart. Another one was still embedded in her arm.

The PJ dragged himself on top of her and shielded her with his body.

"Last stand," he muttered. "Funny how by the time it comes to that, you're never actually standing."

Then he glanced down at her open eyes. "Oh. Didn't realize you were still conscious. Last stand for me, I mean. I'll make sure it isn't yours."

He laid his palm down on her back. It was warm. Comforting.

Catalina's vision kept blurring and the PJ was blocking her line of sight, but she could see some figures approaching them.

"The woman's a civilian," the PJ said. His voice carried on the still air, but his tone was calm as if he was having a perfectly normal conversation. "Just an ordinary good Samaritan. Leave her here. She doesn't know anything. I didn't even tell her my name."

Another man's voice spoke. If the PJ was cool, this man was ice cold. "We know. We've been observing from a distance. And we've seen some *fascinating* things. Her resistance to your power— her general lack of fear— her physical strength. We're certainly not leaving her. She's the perfect subject for 2.0."

There was a brief silence. Then all the hazy figures flinched back. One let out a hoarse scream of sheer terror, then spun around and ran away. A moment later, two more followed him, stumbling and arms flailing, apparently caught in the grip of total panic.

The man with the cold voice spoke again. "I'm impressed. My operatives all underwent intensive fear-resistance training. However, I anticipated that you might get to some of them anyway. That's why

I brought as many men as I did. The three I have left should be more than enough to deal with one partially paralyzed, unarmed renegade."

The PJ replied coolly, "Send them over, and we'll see about that."

"It would be interesting to see what you can manage in that state. However, in the interest of expediting this, I think I'll just give you another dose."

There was snap of fingers, then a faint *whump* of compressed air. Catalina felt the PJ whip around. His hand brushed against her shoulder as he yanked something from his side and threw it back. One of the figures yelped in pain. Then the PJ gave a long sigh and slumped down on top of her. His breathing was even and deep, his hair soft against her cheek.

The figures moved forward, coming closer and closer. Catalina blinked hard, trying to clear her vision. The name on the building in front of her swam into view. She'd collapsed right in front of Protection, Inc.

*Too bad no one's home,* she thought dizzily. *Right now, we could really use a bodyguard.*

Everything went black.

# CHAPTER TWO

*Shane*

Even before he opened his eyes, Shane Garrity knew where he was. He knew by the slight chill in the air— the hum of the air conditioner— the government-issue thin mattress he lay on— and most of all the scent, the sterile cleanness of air stripped of all but a faint odor of antiseptic. He'd lived in that air. He'd dreamed of that air. The smell of it made his stomach turn.

He wondered what had happened to that gorgeous paramedic who had refused to leave him, then carried him over her shoulders for an entire city block. For a woman her size, it had been an amazing feat of strength. For anyone, it had been an amazing feat of heroism. He hoped to hell that Dr. Elihu had just been fucking with him when he'd said they'd take her too.

Shane almost opened his eyes to look for her, then forced himself to lie still, not betraying that he was awake. If they did have the paramedic, he'd rescue her along with himself. He'd escaped once. He could escape again. All he needed to do was gather information and wait for the perfect opportunity to make his move.

He assessed his physical condition. He had a splitting headache, thanks to the unholy combination of a recent concussion and a double dose of tranquilizers, and felt dizzy and slightly nauseated. The familiar pain of cracked ribs stabbed into his side every time he inhaled. But he didn't seem to have any major injuries. He wasn't at peak condition, but he could still fight.

He was covered with a blanket, so he risked tensing the muscles of his legs and feet. The paralysis was gone and he could feel that his panther was back, so the drugs had worn off. He could shift now— but they must know that. He wasn't strapped down or chained up, which had to mean he was locked in.

Soft footsteps approached. He felt the body heat of someone leaning over him. A pair of fingers touched beneath his jaw, seeking for his pulse.

Shane grabbed the person's wrist and twisted it behind their back. In an instant, they were face-down on the floor with him kneeling over them, holding both their arms in a joint-lock.

"Ow!"

Both *her* arms. She was face-down, but he didn't need to see her face to recognize the paramedic. Her silky hair, small but sturdy body, and smooth skin were unmistakable. He'd have known her from touch alone.

He released her immediately. "Sorry. I thought you were an enemy."

They were alone in one of those small rooms that he knew all too well. Two narrow cots. No other furniture. Sterile white walls. Sterile white light. One closed door leading out— that would be locked from the outside and reinforced with steel— and one open door leading to a tiny bathroom.

The paramedic scrambled up, her thick black hair swinging. "Sorry I startled you. I thought you were unconscious. I've been checking your vital signs every ten minutes since I woke up myself."

"I know—" Shane began. Then she lifted her head, and their eyes met.

*She's the one,* hissed his panther.

Shane felt like he'd leaped out of a plane and forgotten to put on his parachute. He was in free-fall, his heart slamming into his chest with a mixture of exhilaration and dread.

He had no doubt that his panther was right. The brave paramedic was his mate. It seemed impossible that he hadn't realized it before. Sure, he'd been drugged then, his panther suppressed. But he still should have known. Of course this fearless woman was his mate. She was what he used to be— someone who'd lay down their life to rescue a stranger, without so much as a second thought. What other woman could he possibly love?

*My mate,* he thought again, lost in wonder.

This woman was his mate, and he hadn't even thought he had one. She was the other half of his soul, and he hadn't thought he had a soul any more, either. He loved her, and he didn't even know her name. If he lost her, it would break him in a way he'd never believed he could be broken.

For the briefest of moments, he was happier than he'd been in years—happier than he'd been in his entire life. His mate was with him at last. It felt so *right.*

Then fear took over.

He'd spent ten years parachuting into combat zones, and his mate was in the closest place to Hell that he'd ever known.

*"She's the perfect subject for 2.0,"* Dr. Elihu had said.

If Apex went through with that, they'd destroy his beautiful, heroic mate.

He had to protect her, but the last time he'd been here, he'd failed to protect anyone.

It was only because of him that she was here at all.

And if he revealed what she meant to him, it would be used against them both. The only way to protect her was to pretend that he didn't care about her.

Shane didn't let emotions get the better of him. He scared other people. Nothing scared him. He fought back against an intensity of love and terror that threatened to overwhelm him, ruthlessly crushing the feelings that would do nothing but compromise his combat fitness.

But the more he suppressed his emotions, the worse he felt physically. A stab of pain went right through his chest, like he'd been shot in the heart. Agony spiked through his head with every throb of his pulse. He broke out in a cold sweat. The room tilted around him, then started to blur.

"Put your head between your knees." A familiar pair of gentle but strong hands pushed him into position. "Take a deep breath. Okay, good. Now take another. Good. Keep going."

Shane breathed deeply until the dizziness faded and the pain eased.

*Keep calm,* he told himself. *You can't protect her if you're not fit yourself.*

When he was certain his voice would be steady, he said, "Sorry. Tranquilizers and concussions are a bad mix."

Her fingers were on his throat again. This time he let her take his pulse. "You should lie down again."

"Nah. I'd rather sit." He raised his head.

This time he got a better look at her. He'd been attracted to her when he'd first seen her, even before he'd known she was his mate. But back then he'd had to focus on immediate survival. This time he had a chance to drink her in.

She was short but not slim, with a body made up of soft curves and strong muscle. Her breasts swelled against her T-shirt and her upper arms stretched out the sleeves. He knew exactly how good she felt, pillowy in some places and resilient in others, because he'd had his arm around her shoulders and his body pressed against hers. He longed to reach out and put his arm around her again…

*Stop that,* he told himself. *Touch her in here, and you might as well put a gun to her head.*

Still, there was no harm in looking. Her hair was black as night and sleek as satin, cut to chin-length. It had slid across his skin like water when she'd lifted him. Her skin was smooth and brown, her eyes a deeper brown with golden highlights. He couldn't help smiling as he looked at her, from her rosy lips to her luscious body to her very decided chin.

Her gaze followed his, and he knew she'd spotted him checking her out. With the hint of laughter trembling in her voice, she said, "You must be feeling better. Take off your shirt."

He wanted to keep that amused look on her face a little longer, so he joked, "That's sudden. Normally women at least want to know my name first."

"Normally I don't go to strange places with strange men I met in dark alleys," she replied, playing along. Then the joking fell away. He already knew how brave she was, so it made a different kind of pain go through his chest at the quick flash of fear he saw in her eyes as she spoke. "Can you tell me what's going on? Who are these people? Why are they after you? Why did they kidnap me? What's 2.0?"

Shane took another deep breath. He had to tell her something, but he couldn't tell her everything. The entire story wasn't necessary, and would only frighten her more.

*Liar,* his panther hissed. *You don't want to tell her because you don't want her to know.*

Shane ignored the beast inside of him. "First, I want you to promise me something. I've been here before. I know how these people work. I can get you out of here, but you have to promise to do exactly what I say. If I wake you up in the middle of the night and tell you to run, you don't ask me what's going on or look for your shoes. You just run."

"So you're telling me I should sleep with my shoes on." She spoke lightly, but he could see that she was giving his request serious consideration.

"That might not be a bad idea. Do you promise?"

In the heartbeat it took her to respond, he wished he could rewind the last few minutes and do everything differently. He'd done nothing to inspire confidence, and everything to seem frightening and dangerous. How could she trust him when she didn't even know who he was?

How could she trust him if he told her *what* he was?

"I promise," she said.

He could hear in her voice that she didn't make promises she didn't intend to keep. His heart lifted with relief. "Okay. Thanks."

"You're welcome. Now *I'm* going to give *you* an order." She jerked her thumb at him. "Your shirt. Off."

Shane grasped the hem of his T-shirt, then stopped. "How are *you* feeling? You were tranquilized too."

She gave a flip of her hand, brushing off the question. "Fine. Seriously. I only got one dose. You had two. Also, I didn't get hit over the head. Now tell me what's going on."

"All right. I'll tell you while you examine me." Shane pulled off his shirt and dropped it on the floor. "What's your name?"

"Catalina Mendez."

That sounded familiar. He rummaged through his mind, trying to place it, and then thought, *Catalina the paramedic. Catalina whose phone didn't work in America.*

"Ellie McNeil's friend?" Shane asked.

"Yes!" Catalina exclaimed. "How do you know her?"

"I'm Shane Garrity. I work with her—" *Her mate.* "Her boyfriend, Hal Brennan."

"Shane the hot bodyguard?" Catalina blurted out, then clapped her hand to her mouth. "Oh my God. I can't believe I just said that. I'm— Uh— I blame the tranquilizers. People think sedatives just sedate you, but sometimes they make you babble. Obviously."

Shane didn't bother pointing out that the tranquilizer had long since worn off. "*Ellie* called me 'the hot bodyguard?'"

"Not you in particular," Catalina said indignantly, as if defending her friend's honor. "She said all the bodyguards were hot, except for the girls— I mean, probably the girls are hot too, she never said they weren't, but since she was telling me and I'm only into guys, she didn't mention whether they were hot or not."

"The girls are hot," Shane said. It wasn't something he thought about much—Destiny and Fiona were like sisters to him. But Catalina was adorable when she got wound up, so he couldn't resist winding her up a little more.

Catalina's cheeks darkened in an intense blush. "Good to know. Now please pretend we didn't just have this conversation. Tell me where it hurts."

She felt all over his belly and sides, while he shook his head. Then she prodded him in the ribcage, right where the worst pain was.

Shane winced. "There."

Now she was back to business. The blush faded. "Does it hurt when you take a deep breath?"

"Yes."

"*Can* you take a deep breath, even though it hurts?"

Shane demonstrated. "Yes."

"Can you taste blood in your mouth?"

"No."

She prodded his chest some more. "I don't have a stethoscope, so this'll have to be old school. Breathe deeply."

Catalina pressed her ear to his chest. Shane forgot to breathe. There she was, with her head against his bare chest and her silky hair touching his skin. If they'd been lying down together, after making love or about to fall asleep, she might rest her head on his chest like that...

She cleared her throat. "Breathe. Hot bodyguard."

He was startled into a laugh. "Ow."

"Did *that* hurt?"

"Yeah." He breathed until she lifted her head, satisfied.

"Your lungs sound fine," she announced. "Your heart rate's good. You've got three cracked ribs. That is, I think they're just cracked, not broken. I couldn't say for sure without x-rays."

"I think so too. Though they might've been broken when you found me." Once the words were out of his mouth, he wished he could take them back. He hadn't meant to hint around like that, but there was something about her that made him reluctant to hide things from her. That made him blurt out the truth whether he'd planned to or not.

He couldn't tell whether it was because she was his mate or because she was so forthright herself. Either way, it made him uncomfortable. He had a lot that he needed to hide. Especially from his mate.

"What?" She shook her head. "No, they can't have been. Broken ribs take weeks to heal. You haven't been here *that* long, Sleeping Beauty."

"I liked Hot Bodyguard better."

She poked him again, thankfully in the shoulder this time.

"That didn't hurt," Shane said helpfully.

"Stop being evasive," she said. "We're locked up in a tiny room, there's nowhere to hide. What did you mean, they might have been broken when I found you?"

"Aren't you going to examine my head? I could have a skull fracture."

"Nah, I think your skull's too thick to break." More seriously, she said, "Sure, I'll take a look. But your pupils are equal, you're not disoriented, and you're not throwing up or passing out. The cut looked shallow, and it's not bleeding any more. I'd be surprised if you had a fracture. Also, you're still dodging my question."

"No. I'm answering it." He turned his head, presenting her with the bloody side. "Look at the cut on my head. Really look at it. You might have to clean off the blood."

Their eyes met. He could see that she knew she was on the brink of learning something important and dangerous.

"Okay." She got up and walked to the bathroom.

Since her back was turned, Shane took the opportunity to check out the swing of her wide hips and the peach-like outline of her ass. His mate was perfect from every angle, and even more beautiful in motion than sitting still.

Catalina returned with a wet washcloth. She sat down beside him and rubbed at the place where he'd been cut. The water was warm and her hands were gentle, and it would have felt good if he didn't know what was coming. He knew what she saw— a mostly-healed cut, looking like it had been inflicted days rather than hours ago— when the motion of her hands stopped.

"That's impossible. We can't have been here that long." She glanced at her watch. "Unless they messed with my watch… But I'd feel different if I'd been unconscious for days, I'm sure I would!"

"It's not your watch. It's me." He held her gaze, willing her to believe the evidence of her own eyes. "Those cracked ribs will be completely healed in a day or two. Same as the cut on my head. Same as why one tranquilizer dart paralyzed you almost instantly and knocked you unconscious a minute later, but it took two to knock me out. Maybe more than two. I'm not sure how many times I was hit before you found me."

He watched the flicker of reactions play across her pretty face, from disbelief to acceptance to curiosity. "Is that why those people grabbed you?"

"Yeah. Well, that's part of it."

She was quick to catch on. "They wanted me as a subject— like, an experimental subject? Were you one too? Is that how you can scare people just by looking at them?"

"Yeah."

"Is it a government experiment to create the ultimate soldier?" Catalina asked excitedly.

Shane was very conscious of the panther within him as he spoke. He controlled his voice to make sure it had none of his animal's hiss. "It was an experiment to create the ultimate *predator*. 2.0 must be their second try at the ultimate predator process. I went through 1.0. I can terrify people and I can sneak up on them without being noticed. I heal fast, and I move fast, and I'm stronger than I was before. And I can turn into a panther."

"No way!" She looked thrilled. It made his heart sink. "And I get to do it too!"

"No, you don't. I won't let them."

"But…" Catalina frowned, her enthusiasm dying down. "I mean, it's not all right that they kidnapped us. Talk about not getting consent for treatment! But being an ultimate predator sounds great. Fast healing, special powers, and you get to turn into a panther! Seriously, you can do that?"

*Show her,* his panther suggested.

For once, he and his panther were on the same page. "Yeah. I'll show you. Just give me a second."

He went into the bathroom, closed the door, and stripped. Then he wrapped a thin white towel around his waist and came back out.

Catalina looked him over with open appreciation. Mischievously, she asked, "'Panther' isn't slang for something else, is it?"

Shane didn't know how she kept managing to make him laugh. It made him realize how little he'd done it in the last couple years. His chuckle came out rusty, like he'd almost forgotten how. "No. I didn't want to rip up my jeans. Watch."

He closed his eyes and focused on being a predator.

*To hunt, to kill, to lurk unseen, to pad silently after his prey, to blend into the darkness and become one with it...*

The panther opened his yellow eyes. Now he could scent Catalina, from the aroma of green apple shampoo lingering in her hair to her own individual scent. His hearing was more acute, allowing him to catch the accelerating rhythm of her heartbeat.

*She's afraid,* he thought. *I should shift back.*

Then she walked right up to him. No trace of fear showed in her face as her hand came down to stroke his fur.

"Wow," she breathed.

*She's excited,* his panther corrected. The big cat sounded smug. *Of course she is. She's our mate.*

Catalina scratched behind his ears. It felt surprisingly good. No one had ever done that before. No one had ever touched his panther at all, except to perform experiments or chain him up.

He found himself turning his head to give her better access. She obligingly kept scratching. He shouldn't have been able to relax, imprisoned again and with the threat of death or worse hanging over his mate, but he did. A strange vibration began to thrum within his chest, making an audible rumble.

*What the hell is that?* Shane wondered.

He hadn't meant to ask his panther, but the big cat replied anyway. *It's called purring.*

There was a distinct subtext of *you idiot* in his panther's tone.

*Okay,* Shane admitted. *I guess I deserved that.*

His panther— and Shane himself, to be honest— would have been content to let the ear-scratching continue indefinitely. But Shane didn't know how long they'd be allowed to stay alone together, and there were things he had to tell Catalina before someone else got to her first.

He closed his eyes and concentrated on human things.

*How to field-strip an M4 carbine. How to seal a sucking chest wound. How to survive if your parachute fails to open.*

Shane opened his eyes as a man.

Catalina still had her fingers in his hair. It felt so good that he didn't know if he could stand to move aside. He felt a stab of mingled relief and regret when she yanked them away.

"Oops," she said. "Sorry. Hope you didn't mind me taking liberties with your ears."

"It's all right when I'm a panther."

"When you're a panther," she echoed delightedly. "Shane, that was the most amazing thing I've seen in my entire life. And I've seen a lot of amazing things. And—" Her gaze strayed downward. "Ha! I'm seeing another one now."

For a moment, he had no idea what she meant. Then he realized that he was naked. He'd spent too much time in barracks to be embarrassed by nudity, but he didn't dare spend one more second naked with his mate. He was sure he had the self-control not to touch her— well, pretty sure— but if she touched him, all bets were off. And she definitely looked like she wanted to.

He gritted his teeth. He ought to be flattered and happy that she was so obviously into him, but under the circumstances, it was nothing but frustrating. Not only could he not do anything about it without putting her at even greater risk, he couldn't even admit his own attraction.

She was strong and brave and kind, but she was also honest. Everything she thought and felt showed on her face. And while their captors might exploit it if they believed that she had an unrequited crush on him, that was nothing to what they'd do if they discovered that he loved her. If they ever learned that he felt more toward her than the basic responsibility any airman would have for a fellow prisoner, all they'd have to do to keep him in line was threaten her. The only way he could protect her was to pretend he didn't care about her.

"Just a sec." He hastily wrapped the towel back around his waist, went to the bathroom, and put his jeans on. Then he returned and sat back down on the floor. Belatedly, he pulled his shirt on too.

Catalina was still grinning. "I can't believe it. You really are that gorgeous panther!"

Inside his head, his panther once again began to purr.

Shane was torn between relief that his mate liked his panther, and dismay that he'd accidentally convinced her that being an ultimate predator was the coolest thing ever. "Listen to me, Catalina. We have to get out of here. *Before* they do anything irrevocable to you. It's not what you think."

She didn't look entirely convinced. "What's the downside?"

His heart lurched. But he'd walked right into the question. He had to answer.

"I didn't volunteer." He made sure his voice sound cool and calm and distant, though he felt none of those things. His heart was hammering so hard that he half-expected her to hear it.

"I was on a combat search and rescue mission when I was captured," Shane went on. "Not by the enemy— well, not by the enemy we were supposed to be fighting. By this place. It's called Apex. It's a black ops agency. They picked me because they thought I was strong enough to have a shot at surviving the ultimate predator process. They were right, but just barely. It nearly killed me. Apex held me for a year before I escaped. By the time I got loose, I'd been declared killed in action. And I might as well have been. My entire life was over. Nobody who knew me before has any idea I'm still alive."

Shane's teammates at Protection, Inc. knew that much of his story. Hal knew the most, because he'd been involved in some of it. But even Hal didn't know all of it. And all of them knew not to ask for more details. Shane couldn't imagine telling anyone the whole story— not even his mate.

Especially not his mate.

Then he felt a warmth penetrate his chill. Catalina had put her hand on his shoulder. "Shane, I'm so sorry. It must have been terrible."

He jerked aside. Pulling away from her felt like ripping off a bandage. Shane wished he could let her touch him, but it was just too dangerous. "No shit."

The flash of hurt in her eyes made him feel even worse. He had to keep his distance, but he didn't have to be an asshole about it. Awkwardly, he muttered, "Ultimate predator is bad news. I was lucky to survive it. It's a lot more likely to kill you than it is to give you powers. Trust me, you don't want it."

"It didn't sound like they were going to give me a choice," Catalina said.

"They have to run tests on you first, to tailor the process to your body. It'll take about a week. But I promise, I'll break us out before then. This time next week, you'll be home."

To his relief, she seemed to accept this. "With one hell of a story. I can't wait to tell Ellie!" Then she frowned. "Can I? Does she know you can turn into a panther? Does Hal know?"

"Hal knows. He can turn into a bear." Shane enjoyed her gasp of delighted surprise. She had the best smile. It made his heart lift.

"No way!"

"Way. Everyone at Protection, Inc. is a shifter. But not like I am. They were born that way. Except—" Shane cut himself off before he blurted out someone else's secret. Smoothly, he went on, "Except they keep it a secret, of course. The entire existence of shifters is a secret. But now that you know, you'll have to ask Ellie to tell you the uncensored version of how she and Hal got together. She left out a lot."

"I *definitely* can't wait." Then her warm brown eyes narrowed thoughtfully. "You know, Ellie's going to notice that I'm missing. And I assume your buddies are going to notice that you are. Are you even going to get a chance to break us out before they break in?"

Shane had been wondering that himself. But he couldn't get sidetracked by wishful thinking. "They'll be looking for us, for sure. But Apex is good at covering their tracks. We can't count on rescue. We have to bet on escape."

"Do you already have an escape plan?"

"Sort of. Subject to contact with the enemy."

She nodded, obviously familiar with the saying, *No battle plan survives contact with the enemy.* "What is it?"

"It'll work better if you don't know about it in advance. Sorry. You'll have to—"

There was a familiar *clunk* of the steel door's deadbolts sliding back.

"Trust me," he breathed.

The door opened. Dr. Elihu stood in the doorway. The sight of the heavyset man in the white coat gave Shane the same sickening inner lurch as the scent of the air.

*Rip his throat out.* Shane's panther sent him a hot red wash of blood-lust.

*Not now.* Shane kept firm control on his panther. *Later.*

Dr. Elihu was flanked by guards with tranquilizer pistols and Tasers. If Shane so much as twitched in a suspicious way, he'd be subdued in an instant. And that would do no good for either him or Catalina.

*Rip his throat out,* demanded his panther. *NOW.*

The urge to kill was overwhelming, but Shane forced himself to stay cool.

*Want to be chained up again?* Shane asked his panther. *Patience. We're still lying in wait. The kill comes later.*

*Lying in wait,* the big cat hissed in reluctant agreement. *We can wait. But not forever...*

"Long time no see, Dr. Elihu," said Shane.

"How pleasant to have you back with us," returned the doctor. "I trust you enjoyed your time off?"

"I enjoyed it so much, I was thinking of making it permanent."

The doctor made a tch-tch noise. "I'm afraid your vacation time is used up, Garrity. It's back on the job for you." Then he turned to Catalina. "Come with me, Mendez. I'll give you a tour of your new workplace."

"Sure you wouldn't rather have me do that?" Shane inquired.

Shane caught a flash of pure venom in the doctor's tone as he replied, "Have a little more time off, Garrity. Relax."

Catalina glanced at Shane, obviously looking for a cue. Dropping the sarcasm, he said, "Go with him, or he'll have the guards drag you."

*Enough lying and waiting,* spat out his panther. *Kill him before he hurts our mate!*

The big cat's protective fury— and his own— made Shane's vision haze crimson. But he clamped down on his beast and himself, not letting a flicker of emotion show on his face or body, as he watched as his mate walk out the door with the man he'd sworn to kill.

# CHAPTER THREE

## *Catalina*

Catalina hated to walk out the door, leaving Shane behind. Her stomach clenched in an unpleasant flutter that was starting to feel all too familiar. But she was less afraid for herself than she was concerned for him. Cool as he'd seemed when he'd traded sarcastic remarks with the doctor, she could tell that it shook him to be trapped in that place. She felt awful leaving him alone, imprisoned in an empty room with nothing to occupy his mind but his pain and his memories.

The heavy steel door locked behind her. She stood in a corridor like those in hospitals, all white walls and fluorescent light strips, flanked by the creepy doctor and a bunch of guards.

"So, I'm going to be working for you now?" Catalina asked as they began to walk down the corridor. "Isn't this a lot of trouble to go to just to hire a paramedic?"

Dr. Elihu gave her an oily smile. "We don't want you for a paramedic any more than we wanted Shane because he knows how to parachute. We're offering you a chance to serve your country in a much more significant fashion."

"Doing what?"

"Don't play coy. Garrity must have briefed you." The doctor gestured for her to turn left, into another corridor.

Catalina tried to memorize the doors and branching corridors as she passed them. The place would be easier to get lost in than even the notoriously mazelike Santa Martina Central Hospital.

"Not really," she said. "He's pretty closed-mouthed. And you shouldn't just leave him in that room. He needs to see a doctor."

"He's already been examined," Dr. Elihu replied. "His injuries don't require attention. Soon you too will have accelerated healing capabilities."

"If I don't drop dead!"

The doctor gave her a bland stare. "Sounds like Garrity's mouth wasn't *completely* closed."

Catalina scowled, wishing she wasn't so prone to blurting out exactly what she was thinking. No wonder Shane hadn't been willing to tell her his plan. "I hope you don't want to make me into a spy. I'd be the worst one ever."

"No, we'll tailor your assignments to your capabilities."

Catalina didn't feel remotely reassured. "Like what? What have you been making Shane do for you?"

"Missions to support the best interests of America."

*Black ops,* Shane had said. And his eyes had gone bleak as a frozen lake.

"Assassinations, right?" Catalina demanded. "He was a hero— he *saved* people—and you forced him to become a hit man!"

The doctor didn't so much as blink, though her voice had echoed off the white walls. "War isn't pretty. And Garrity chose to enlist."

"He didn't choose this!"

Dr. Elihu's emotionless gaze reminded her of a snake. "He had options. He still does. Just as you do."

"So I can leave?" Catalina inquired. "Great! Show me the exit."

"You may consider yourself drafted. I'm not going to make it easy for you to desert. But all soldiers have that option. So will you, in time. But like all choices, it will have a price."

"What's the price?"

"Garrity can tell you. Though of course, it'll only be relevant to you if you don't *drop dead*." The doctor mockingly imitated her inflections. Catalina wanted to punch him. "But since he informed you of the mortality rate of ultimate predator 1.0, you'll be happy to hear that 2.0 is much safer."

"How much safer?"

"We estimate a survival rate of up to fifty percent."

Catalina's stomach lurched again, then steadied. Fifty-fifty wasn't bad odds. 1.0 had apparently been even more dangerous than that, but Shane had survived it. And she was hardly a stranger to risk-taking. She'd flown into disaster zones and treated gunshot victims when the people who shot them might still be around. In Loredana, she'd crawled into a partially collapsed building to treat a man who was still pinned inside, knowing that they'd both be killed if there was an aftershock. He'd survived, and afterward the doctors had said it had been thanks to her. Some risks were worth taking.

She remembered the thick velvet of the panther's fur, his sleek muscles and sense of controlled power. Catalina didn't want to want something that was being forced on her, might kill her, and came with the price of being enslaved by an evil black ops agency. But she did want it. She'd always dreamed of having super-powers.

"And if it works, I'll be able to turn into a panther?" she asked. "And terrify people just by looking at them?"

The doctor pursed his narrow lips. "You'll be able to do *something* that a predator can do. It might not be the same as Garrity's powers. As for turning into a panther, that's up to him."

"What do you mean?"

"He has to bite you," said the doctor. "I suggest that you persuade him to do it. The enhanced healing abilities will raise your odds of surviving the ultimate predator process. Without them, the odds will be worse than fifty percent. Perhaps much worse."

They took another turn. Catalina had lost track of how many they'd taken, distracted by thoughts of super-powers and shapeshifting and black ops and her own possible imminent death. And of Shane, the hot bodyguard. The hot bodyguard who could turn into a panther.

She wouldn't have thought anything could distract her from *holy shit I've been kidnapped,* not to mention *holy shit panther,* but Shane himself had done the trick. It wasn't just how gorgeous he was, especially in the nude, with his long legs and lean muscle and fine bone structure. It was the heat that had risen up from his body. It was his scent of clean masculine sweat, so unexpectedly human in that sterile room. It was the grace of his body in motion, the irresistible strength of his hands, the velvety softness of his hair, and the unexpected beauty of those blue eyes in that hard face.

But more than that, she was drawn to *him.* They hadn't had much time together, but Catalina was used to living her life in brief, intense encounters. She often had only a few minutes to save a life, and then a few more in the ambulance before she turned her patients over to the ER, never to see them again. But she'd had patients she'd known for fifteen minutes and would remember for the rest of her life, and she was sure that many of them would never forgot those crucial minutes they'd spent with her.

In the little time she'd had with Shane, he'd tried to protect her any way that he could, whether it was trying to scare her away or calmly explaining what was going on or shielding her with his own body. He'd respected her abilities, which was more than she could say for a lot of the men she'd worked with. His cool reserve was smoking hot, and the glimpses of vulnerability she'd seen tugged at her heart.

But, of course, he wasn't into her. She hadn't missed how quickly he'd gotten dressed after he'd caught her admiring his body, how he'd jerked away from her impulsive touch on his shoulder, and how he'd dropped even the joke of flirting with her once he'd spotted that for her, it wasn't only joking.

*Hot bodyguard who'd risk his life for me, but wouldn't ever kiss me,* she thought. *Maybe it's for the best. Right now I need protecting more than I need kissing.*

The same reckless part of her that wanted to be an ultimate predator said, *I'd rather have the kissing.*

*I'd rather have both,* Catalina admitted. Then she firmly told herself, *Be happy you have one.*

It was going to be awkward being stuck with Shane in that little room, though. At least they had the bathroom to change in. She'd just do her best to keep her thoughts off her face and not embarrass him. And also, not stare at him. Not flirt with him, even playfully. And definitely not touch him again. He obviously hadn't liked that at all.

*Except when he was a panther,* she recalled, suppressing a grin. *I always did have a way with cats.*

"Here we are." Dr. Elihu escorted her into a room full of medical testing equipment, some of which she recognized and some of which she didn't. "Have a seat."

Catalina warily sat on the examination table. The guards stayed while

Dr. Elihu summoned a nurse to take her blood pressure and temperature, and then to draw her blood.

"People will notice I'm gone," she said. "They're going to look for me."

Dr. Elihu replied, "Women go missing all the time. Especially when they do reckless things like walk alone at night. No one will be surprised that your disregard of basic safety finally caught up to you."

Catalina couldn't decide which made her more furious, that he was lecturing her on safety after he'd kidnapped her, or that he was probably right that her family would believe that she'd been murdered. No amount of super-powers would be worth that.

*Shane will break me out,* she reassured herself. *That's what PJs do—they rescue people.*

That thought got her through an entire day of medical exams. She got a CT scan, an MRI, a bone scan, full-body X-Rays, and an EKG. They tested her vision, her hearing, her pulmonary function, her reflexes, and even her ability to smell, taste, and touch.

At first she was intrigued by the tests and machines she'd read about but never personally encountered before, like the PET scan, and the ones she'd never even heard of, like tensiomyography. Then she got bored. Then she started wondering again about Shane. How was he holding up, alone in that little room with nothing to do? Or were they running tests on him in some different part of the building?

Finally, she couldn't take it any more. She stepped off the treadmill they'd used for a stress test of her heart and demanded, "What are you doing with Shane?"

Dr. Elihu gave her a long look before he replied, as if he'd learned something about her because she'd asked that question. "Nothing bad. And that will continue... So long as you cooperate."

There went that goddamn stomach flutter again. Catalina had come back from months in a disaster zone, and one day later, she'd been scared more often than she'd been in the last *year*.

"Let me get this straight," she said. "Are you saying that you won't hurt him so long as I toe the line?"

"That is exactly what I said," the doctor replied condescendingly. Then, as if he was making a private joke, he added, "We can skip the test of auditory comprehension; that's obviously perfect."

If there was one thing Catalina hated, it was men patronizing her. If it wasn't for them threatening Shane, she'd have been tempted to haul off and punch him. And the thought of them deliberately hurting Shane made her even angrier. He'd made a career out of risking his life to save others, and his reward had been to be kidnapped and used. And now he was being held hostage to ensure her cooperation.

Hot blood rushed into her face, making her skin feel tight and swollen. She clenched her fists, holding herself back by sheer force of will.

"Now!" Dr. Elihu exclaimed. "Nurse! Quickly!"

The next thing Catalina knew, she was being hustled into some scanner she didn't even recognize. She lay in its narrow tube, silently furious. Her rage only increased when she realized that the doctor had deliberately baited her so he could scan her brain while she was angry.

*Go ahead and make me a predator,* she thought. *Let's see you condescend to a panther that can bite your head off.*

As the scan continued, she cooled off enough to think, *But Shane can bite their heads off, too. Sure, they can hold him at gunpoint. But how do they make him work for them? Do they have guards go with him when they send him out to kill people?*

The scanner slid her out, ending that train of thought. Catalina sat up. "Now what?"

"Now for a very important meeting," said Dr. Elihu. "We're going to introduce you to someone who went through 2.0, just like you will. But we're hoping you won't have the same problems he does."

"What problems?"

"His animal took him over," replied the doctor. "Oh, he's still intelligent. He can follow orders. But otherwise, he's a wild beast in human form. When he comes in, don't make any sudden movements. And whatever you do, don't speak. The guards will stand ready, but he can move very quickly. They might not be able to tranquilize him before he rips out your throat with his teeth."

Catalina snorted in disbelief. "You're just trying to scare me."

"I don't advise that you attempt to test that hypothesis."

"And why am I meeting this guy?"

"So he can get your scent and track you down if you attempt to desert," Dr. Elihu replied coolly. "Now, remember what I said. Don't move, and don't talk."

Catalina was still trying to decide if it was all an elaborate mind game when the doctor picked up a remote control and hit a button. A door slid open, and a man walked in.

The moment she saw him, she knew that the doctor hadn't lied. The man moved with a predatory grace, like Shane's panther trapped in a human body. He didn't walk, he *stalked*, his gaze fixed on her.

Catalina froze instinctively, knowing in her gut that he was a predator and she was prey. She'd never felt anything like that in her life, not even when Shane had used his fear power on her. That fear had been a weapon Shane deliberately deployed; this fear was the natural effect of what this man was.

Her palms prickled with sweat as he approached her. Then she forced herself to be calm and observe. The man was tall and muscular, with black hair and eyes so dark that she couldn't see the difference between his iris and his pupils. His skin was startlingly pale in contrast.

She held her breath as he reached out to her, but all he did was touch her hand.

"Got it," he said.

Catalina almost jumped out of her skin when he spoke. From what Dr. Elihu had said, she hadn't thought the man *could* speak. His words hadn't come out in a growl or snarl or any animal-like noise, but had simply been a man's matter-of-fact report.

He turned around and walked out. Catalina didn't move until the door slid shut behind him. Then the air whooshed out of her lungs, leaving all her muscles feeling like jelly.

"He can find you anywhere now," said Dr. Elihu. "Don't try to run away, unless you want him to come after you."

"I won't," Catalina assured him.

But her mind was racing ahead, imagining being that predator. It was at once horrifying and weirdly tempting. She didn't want to terrify people— she liked people. But she'd always wondered what it would be like to be a cat, like the trio of adorable, fluffy predators that shared her apartment. She loved watching them leap to the tops of her bookcases. That dark-eyed man could jump like a cat, she bet.

*What would it be like…?*

***

It was evening when Dr. Elihu dispatched guards to escort Catalina back to her room. She knew that by checking her watch; she hadn't seen a single window to the outside. The entire walk there, her mind spun with thoughts of escape, of ultimate predators, of shapeshifters, and of Shane. Had they really locked him alone in the room all day?

When the guards opened the door, Shane was sitting on the floor, stretching. His long legs were spread wide, nearly in a split, and he was bent over at the waist with his chest touching the floor. Other than professional athletes, she'd never seen a man his size with that much flexibility.

Unhurriedly, he raised his head. His gaze locked on the guards. They all flinched, and several stumbled back. The others pushed Catalina inside, then quickly slammed the door.

She laughed. "Good one."

"I couldn't resist," Shane said.

His legs were still spread out, giving her a perfect view of his package. She'd already seen it— the real thing, not just the outline— but there was something differently hot about seeing the fabric of his blue jeans stretched tight against his cock. It made her want to sit on his lap with her own jeans on, and rub against him until they had to rip each other's clothes off or come in their pants.

Catalina shook her head fiercely, trying to knock out the fantasies. No sense adding unbearable sexual frustration to her situation. "Feeling better?"

"Uh-huh." He pulled his legs in and sat cross-legged on the floor, which was almost as good a view as she'd gotten with his legs stretched out. She tried not to look at anything below his waist. "Maybe it was just as well I had a day with nothing to do but rest and stretch."

"Were you stuck here the whole time?"

He nodded. "They're punishing me for running away. Torture by boredom. What did they do to you? Just tests, right?"

"Right…"

He caught her hesitation. "Tell me exactly what happened and where you went. Every detail that you can remember, down to the layout of the building."

"So you can plan our escape?"

"Yeah. I've done it before."

She had no doubt that he could. He looked like he could do *anything*. What would he be like in bed? He could probably take a woman to places she'd never even imagined...

*Stop that,* she told herself.

Trying not to look at him too much, she began recounting her day, starting with her conversation with Dr. Elihu. She skipped the part about Shane's probable career as an assassin, since that had to be a painful topic, but asked him, "What did Dr. Elihu mean when he said you could tell me the price of desertion? Did he just mean they'd kill me if I tried to escape?"

Shane brushed a strand of black hair from his forehead. Catalina was doing her best not to be hypnotized by his body, but it was challenging when every single part of him was so completely worth looking at. His hands were long-fingered and deft, with the tiny scars over the knuckles you got by practicing martial arts or fighting for real. Or both.

"No," Shane replied, jerking her attention back to the conversation. "He meant that once you undergo the ultimate predator process, if you survive, you need regular medical care to keep your body from rejecting it."

"Like an organ transplant?" Catalina said. "You have to take immune-suppressing medication?"

"More like dialysis," Shane replied. "There's a machine that takes out your blood and does something to it, and then transfuses it back. Dr. Elihu wouldn't tell me how it works. He said I couldn't understand it, but he was just being a dick. He wanted to make sure I wouldn't be able to have it done anywhere else, so I'd have to keep coming back here."

Catalina frowned. "But you escaped. Did you figure out how to have it done? Or are you due for a treatment?"

"Neither." Shane didn't say anything more for a long time, letting an uncomfortable silence stretch out. Finally, he said, "I don't need it any more. But that doesn't apply to you. If you go through the process, you'll be stuck here."

There was obviously a lot he wasn't telling her, but it seemed hard enough for him to have said what he had. Catalina decided not to press him farther, and returned to her account of her day in the lab. He listened intently, his gaze distant, as if he was memorizing everything.

Then his eyes snapped into sharp focus when she described her meeting with the man who could supposedly track her down if she escaped.

"Was that true?" she asked. "Or was Dr. Elihu playing mind games?"

"Both, probably," Shane replied. "Any shifter can track by scent. But there's ways around that."

"What about getting taken over by your animal? True? Or mind games?"

Shane's expression was as bleak as it had been when he'd mentioned black ops. "That could definitely happen."

*How do you know?* Catalina wondered. *Because Dr. Elihu told you? Or because it nearly happened to you?*

In a distinct *Let's change the subject* voice, he said, "Want to have dinner? They brought in some MREs."

He pointed to the corner. It now contained two packages of military rations, plus two stacks of new clothes. She went over and inspected the clothes. They'd both gotten a week's worth of jeans, T-shirts, pajamas, and underwear, and Catalina had additionally gotten several bras.

She hastily dropped a T-shirt over the bras and panties, and scooped up an MRE as a distraction. "Are these things really as gross as everyone says?"

"You tell me. I'm used to them."

He opened the packages and assembled the chemical heater. While he took them into the bathroom to run water into them to start the heater, Catalina read the instructions. When he came out, she was laughing.

"What's so funny?" He sat down and leaned the packages against the sole of his shoe, making her laugh harder.

She pointed to a diagram of how to heat an MRE, with each part from "heater" to "folded end" neatly labeled. The MRE in the drawing leaned against a rock labeled "rock or something."

Catalina tapped his foot. "'Or something.'"

Shane smiled. "I used to have a T-shirt with that diagram, only it had a lobster instead of a rock."

"A lobster's definitely something."

"Wish I had one now," Shane said. "When I was a kid, I used to trap them and bring them home for my grandma to cook. We'd sit at the kitchen table and eat them with melted butter."

"That sounds fun." She grinned, trying to picture a tiny Shane. It was hard to imagine that utterly adult and masculine man as a little boy. "Were you on vacation, or did your grandma live with you?"

"She lived with me." Shane paused and adjusted the MREs, and Catalina thought that was all he had to say. But to her surprise, he went on, "My father was never in the picture, and my mother died when I was four. My grandmother raised me in a little house on the coast of Maine."

"Is she still there?"

He shook his head. "She died eight years ago. She did get to see me become a PJ, though. She was proud. She'd been in the Air Force herself, as an aircraft technician."

"Did you have other family?" Catalina asked. "Or was it just you and her?"

"Just me and her. My grandfather died before my mom did, and the family had been small to begin with. What about you?"

"I lived with my grandma too," Catalina replied. "Also my grandpa, my parents, an aunt, two brothers, and a sister, all in a room about this size."

Shane glanced around the small room. "Sounds like some barracks I've lived in. Did you ever get an upgrade?"

"Yeah, in middle school we moved into a two-bedroom. By the time I was in high school, we were in a real house. We came over from Mexico— I mean, my parents and grandparents and aunt did, the kids were born here— and the adults worked 24-7 to support us. They wanted us to have a better life than they did."

"They must be proud of you."

"Well— sort of." Catalina sighed. "I'm the baby. I have one brother who's a cardiologist and another who's an immigration lawyer. My sister's a judge. I was supposed to be a doctor or a lawyer or an engineer. But I've never liked sitting still and studying. Becoming a paramedic was hard enough. I can't imagine doing four years of college and then years more of grad school. My family's glad I earn an honest living and it's not as backbreaking as what they had to do, but they really wanted me to get a fancy degree and have my own office."

"And sit down all day, pushing papers and wearing a business suit?"

"You got it."

"That's no life for people like us," Shane said. "Your patients are lucky you didn't do what your family wanted."

Catalina had never looked at it that way before. She was still thinking about that, and also about the "like us," when he unwrapped the MREs and set them before her.

"Take your pick."

She inspected them. They contained packets of candy and crackers, plus main dishes consisting of whitish glop and brownish glop. "What's the difference?"

"Light is chicken, dark is beef," Shane replied. "Or something."

Catalina laughed and took the chicken. Or, more likely, something. Reluctantly, she stuck in her fork and took a bite. "Tastes exactly like it looks."

Shane seemed more pleased with his meal. "Makes me feel like I'm back in the field."

"Could you be a PJ again?" she asked. "I mean, once you get out of here?"

"No. There's no going back."

He didn't explain further, but he didn't seem to mind that she'd asked. For the rest of the meal and some time afterward, they traded stories of their jobs, of close calls and saved lives, and of pranks and silliness on their down time.

*Fun hot bodyguard*, she thought. *I hope we can be friends once all this is over.*

She tried not to think of it as a consolation prize. No matter how fascinating his stories were and how engaged she was in conversation, she couldn't turn off her awareness of how sexy he was. Every time he moved, she was captivated by his power and grace. It was incredibly frustrating to be so close to him, to know that all she'd have to do to touch his warm skin was reach out her hand, and to be unable to do it.

*Untouchable hot bodyguard,* she thought. *Wonder if you already have a girlfriend, or if you're holding out for the perfect woman. Bet you bag a supermodel lawyer with a black belt in kung fu.*

Catalina gritted her teeth in frustration. She and Shane were so compatible. They had similar interests and jobs. He obviously enjoyed talking to her as much as she enjoyed talking to him. They were locked up together in a tiny room, and they hadn't annoyed each other yet.

But you couldn't argue with a lack of sexual attraction. He just wasn't into her like that.

*And that,* she told herself firmly, *was that.*

The time flew by until they were both yawning. When she checked her watch, she was startled to find that it was nearly midnight.

They went to bed in their narrow cots. Shane reached up and flicked off the wall switch. Instead of plunging the room into pitch-black darkness, as she'd expected, it switched to a dim bluish light. She could still see him, his knees bent so his long legs wouldn't dangle off the end of the cot.

"Good night, Shane," she said.

"Good night, Catalina." He turned over and settled in, so all she could see was his velvety black hair. Within a few minutes, his breathing deepened into the even rhythm of sleep.

She lay and listened for a while, wishing she could lie beside him. Her cot felt excruciatingly empty, with every inch of her skin longing to be pressed up against his. But though she was frustrated, she wasn't lonely. Shane was right there with her, only a few feet away, and she'd seen how fast he reacted. If anything happened, he'd be up and ready to protect her.

With that thought to comfort her, she fell asleep.

***

Catalina woke with a start. For a moment, she was completely disoriented, unsure where she was or what time it was. She didn't even know what country she was in. Then memory rushed back in, along with the realization of what had woken her. A man's harsh gasps filled the room.

Her eyes flew open as she sat straight up. But though Shane's breathing sounded as if he was fighting or badly hurt, he lay on his cot with his eyes closed, completely still except for the desperate heaving of his chest. He'd thrown off his blanket, so she could see that all his muscles were tensed and his hands were clenched in fists. Though the room was cold, sweat beaded his face.

Catalina knew better than to touch him. He'd probably lash out instinctively. Instead, she called softly, "Shane?"

He jolted awake instantly, levering himself up on one hand. The other snatched at his hip and closed around empty air instead of the gun he'd probably expected to find. His eyes were colorless in the dim light, and his expression would have frightened her if she didn't know him.

"It's me, Catalina," she said. "I think you were having a nightmare."

"Oh." He sat up and took a few deep breaths. "Thanks for waking me up."

She wanted to put her arm around his shoulders, but he didn't like her touching him. It wouldn't be comforting for him. "Is there anything I can do?"

He opened his mouth like he was going to say something, then closed it and wrapped his arms tight around his chest. He looked like he was holding himself back.

*From doing what?* Catalina wondered.

"No. I'm all right." It was obvious that he wasn't. He sat stiff and tense, with none of his usual grace, hunched over as if he was in physical pain.

"What were you dreaming about?" Catalina asked.

"I don't remember." He stood up. "Go back to sleep. I'm taking a shower."

Catalina lay back down as he walked to the bathroom. She listened to the shower run as she lay there wishing there was something she could do for him. But he didn't want to be touched and he didn't want to talk, so what did that leave?

She wondered about his dream, which she was certain he did remember. He'd been in combat, of course, but that wasn't necessarily it. She'd seen plenty of things that would give some people nightmares, but she never had bad dreams about her work, unless you counted the ones about showing up naked and without her stethoscope. And Shane had said he'd loved being a PJ.

The shower ran and ran. It was still going when she fell asleep.

# CHAPTER FOUR

## *Catalina*

"Catalina. Come on, wake up."

She groggily peeled open her eyes. "What?"

"It's morning." Shane, still in pajamas, was sitting up on his cot. The lights were on. He had faint dark smudges under his eyes, but otherwise he looked as serene as ever. "You should get up and shower."

"Why?"

"If you don't now, you might not get a chance till night time. They keep early hours here."

"Ugh." She rolled out of bed, stumbled to the clothing stack, grabbed a handful of clothes, and made her way to the bathroom. By the time she finished her shower, she was more awake.

Shane went into the bathroom as soon as she left. The shower started running again.

*Clean freak,* she thought, remembering his middle-of-the-night shower. *Well, he* is *part cat. They're always washing.*

The shower was still going when she heard a metallic clunk. The door opened, revealing Dr. Elihu and his security guard escort.

"Where's Garrity?" Dr. Elihu said immediately.

"Taking a shower," Catalina replied. As if he couldn't hear it!

Though you could see the entire room, including under both cots, at a single glance, the doctor took a long, careful look around. Then he jerked his thumb at a guard. "You. Check. The rest of you, cover him."

Catalina hastily stepped out of the line of fire as the guards raised their tranquilizer guns.

The guard Dr. Elihu had indicated warily knocked on the bathroom door. "Garrity?"

There was no response.

"He probably can't hear you," Catalina said.

"Open the door," Dr. Elihu ordered.

The bathroom door didn't lock from the inside. The guard yanked it open, revealing Shane stepping out of the shower, naked and dripping wet. He seemed unperturbed at the guards drawing down on him, not to mention Catalina and the doctor staring at him.

It was a sight glorious enough to wake her up, even at that ungodly hour. She knew she shouldn't stare, but he was just standing there, without so much as a towel in his hand. She forced her gaze away from his big cock and the elegant hollows of his hip bones, up to his perfect six-pack, broad shoulders, and sleek hair. His wet eyelashes framed his piercing eyes, and water outlined every muscle.

"Can I help you?" Shane inquired politely.

The guard slammed the door. But Catalina had seen plenty. And since she'd probably never see it again, she'd just cherish the memory.

"Come with me, Mendez," the doctor ordered. "I have more tests for you."

That day was just like the first, only with different tests and minus the encounter with the dark-eyed man. Once again, she couldn't stop thinking of Shane as she had more blood drawn and ran an obstacle course and did multiple tests measuring her hand-eye coordination. How long were they going to keep him locked up in that room? What was it that haunted his dreams? Was it possible to spontaneously combust from sexual frustration?

The guards returned her that evening. When they opened the door to her room, Shane was down on the floor doing push-ups with his shirt off. The muscles of his back glistened with sweat, and his hair was soaked. He was counting quietly to himself, but stopped and sat up when the door opened.

Two of the guards managed to avert their eyes, but he caught the other four with his predator stare. Two flinched but held steady, one staggered backward, and one actually dropped his tranquilizer gun. The remaining guards instantly leveled their guns at Shane, who hadn't so much as blinked.

"Think of your weapon as an extension of your hand," Shane advised the guard who had dropped his gun. "Then you'll never drop it."

Swearing, the guards slammed the door.

Catalina laughed. "Never not funny."

"I'm glad someone appreciates it," Shane remarked.

Catalina sat on the floor beside him. "Looks like your ribs are doing better. How many push-ups was that?"

"One thousand, eight hundred, and twelve," Shane said. "I'm trying to beat the world record."

"Did you?"

"Got me. The record is two thousand, two hundred, and twenty in one hour. But I don't have a watch."

She held up her hand, showing him hers. "Want me to time you?"

"Nah. I'm worn out."

He didn't look or sound worn out. Catalina bet he could have beat the record. She struggled not to stare at his incredible musculature. He was flushed from exertion, his nipples rose-pink. If she kissed them, they'd taste like salt and harden under her tongue. She fixed her gaze on his face, but his intensity made her feel like he was reading her mind. She hoped he hadn't picked up on her fantasy of licking his chest.

*Spontaneous combustion is a definite possibility,* she thought.

To distract herself, she recounted her day in detail, all the way down to the layout of the corridors. When she finished, she asked, "Learn anything useful?"

"It's all useful. Sooner or later, they'll have to let me out of here." He went to the bathroom, toweled off, and put his shirt back on.

*Oh, well,* she thought. *The view was nice while it lasted. Anyway, he's less distracting now.*

He began to pace the room, restless power in every line of his body. Like a caged animal. Like his panther. His frustration was palpable, infecting her as well. She'd lose her mind if she'd been locked up alone all day in a tiny room with no TV, no books, no music, no games, no pen and paper, no nothing— not even a view.

To distract him and herself, she said, "I see we got some new MREs."

He stopped pacing and picked them up. "Yeah. I hope they're grabbing them randomly, then maybe we'll get some different entrees. The pork and rice was my favorite."

His hope was dashed when they sat down to eat them and discovered that it was once again chicken glop and beef glop. Catalina picked the beef glop for a change, only to discover that it tasted exactly the same as the chicken glop. But she enjoyed being with Shane as much as she had the night before, and that made up for the disgusting food.

He pointed to the one component of her MRE that she hadn't been able to bring herself to try, a "snack bar" that looked like gray cardboard. "Are you going to eat that?"

"It's a sacrifice, but I'll let you have it. Whatever it is."

She flipped it to him. He caught and ate it, though he didn't seem to enjoy it.

"What's it taste like?" she asked.

"Something," he replied, deadpan.

Catalina grinned. "I guess conditions aren't that bad, considering that we were kidnapped. I mean, we could have a bucket instead of a bathroom."

"Yeah, we're living in style," Shane remarked. "I've done way worse."

"Me too," Catalina said, then added, "Not worse than you, I'm sure."

"Ellie said you were living out of a tent for months in Loredana."

"Well, yeah. But not in a combat zone."

"In a disaster zone. Ellie told us all how you crawled into a building that could have collapsed at any second."

"Just doing my job."

"That's not what I heard," Shane remarked. "What I heard was that you were all ordered to stay out until the bracing equipment arrived, but you disobeyed orders and went in anyway."

"Only when we found out that the equipment wouldn't arrive for hours," Catalina protested. "I had to go in— a man was bleeding to death."

Shane's level blue gaze met hers. "I know. You went above and beyond the call."

"Oh." Now she could see the sincere admiration in his eyes. It moved her; unexpectedly, she found her eyes prickling, as if she might cry.

*This is the respect you've always wanted,* she thought. *If a PJ thinks you went above and beyond, that really means something.*

But it wasn't just because Shane was a PJ. It was because he was Shane.

She cared about what he thought of her, not as a PJ, but as a person. She wanted him to respect her— wanted him to like her— wanted him to care about her in a way that he didn't and never would—

The prickling increased. Catalina hastily lowered her gaze, letting her hair swing forward to hide her face, and pulled a piece of something apart with a fork.

She prayed that Shane wouldn't notice anything. If she had to speak, she'd sound choked up. And then he'd ask what was wrong, and she'd have to lie and say it was because she was upset about being kidnapped. She couldn't tell him, "I can't help falling for you, but no matter how brave you think I am, you'll never feel the same way about me, and it's breaking my heart."

Shane stood up. "I'll go wash my hands."

Once she heard the bathroom door click shut and the sink start running, she mopped at her eyes and sniffed hard. By the time he returned, she'd recovered her composure and could re-start the conversation.

When they went to bed, he again fell asleep almost immediately. He hadn't mentioned his nightmare and she hadn't brought it up, but she hadn't forgotten about it. She hoped he'd sleep through the night.

# CHAPTER FIVE

## *Catalina*

If Shane had another nightmare, it didn't wake her up. She slept so soundly that he practically had to drag her out of bed the next morning.

"Do you want a shower or not?" he demanded.

She burrowed back under the covers. "You take yours first."

"Nah, that's not going to work out." He yanked off the blanket. "Shower now, or don't shower till tonight."

She dragged herself out of bed and into the shower. Still half-asleep, she didn't wonder until Shane had vanished into the bathroom why he was so determined that she take the first one. But when Dr. Elihu and the guards showed up ten minutes later, she remembered the morning before and realized that it was so she wouldn't risk having them yank the door open while she was naked.

*He could've just said so,* Catalina thought. *But it was a sweet thought. Sweet, hot, closed-mouthed bodyguard.*

"Shane's in the shower," she told the doctor.

Dr. Elihu ignored her and jerked his thumb at the nearest guard. The guard yanked open the bathroom door.

Shane pulled back the shower curtain and turned off the water. Once again, he stood naked and dripping wet, in full view of everyone in the room and the corridor. But he didn't seem embarrassed at all.

Looking straight at Dr. Elihu, he said, "If you're that eager to see me naked, you could just order me to take off my clothes."

The doctor flushed bright red. "Garrity, shut that door!"

With a catlike smile, Shane unhurriedly closed the bathroom door.

For the rest of the day, which consisted of still yet more medical tests, every now and then Catalina would recall that incident and laugh aloud.

Exasperated, Dr. Elihu finally snapped, "If you're hoping to convince me to drop you from the ultimate predator program on the basis of psychosis, you'll have to do better than inappropriate laughter."

"I was remembering Shane making you blush," Catalina retorted. "It's very appropriate."

"I don't blush," the doctor snapped, and stuck her extra-hard with a hypodermic needle.

When she was returned to the room that evening, Shane again seemed to have been exercising. He was barefoot and shirtless, his chest glistening with sweat, crouched on the floor like some great cat about to pounce. The guards didn't give him a chance to look up and terrify them, but shoved Catalina inside and slammed the door.

"Hi, honey, I'm home!" Catalina said brightly.

Shane sat up, playing along. "How was your day at the office?"

"My boss is an asshole. Otherwise, not too bad. How about you, how was your day?"

"Being a homemaker isn't all it's cracked up to be," he replied, deadpan. "I'm thinking of re-entering the work force."

She sat down on her cot. "What were you doing when I came in?"

"Karate. Did you ever study martial arts?"

She shook her head. "My family couldn't afford lessons when I was young, and I never got around to it later."

He tilted his head, regarding her with those cool predator's eyes. "But you've fought. I can tell. What was it, street fighting?"

"Sort of. I was just a teenager."

"I enlisted when I was eighteen," Shane pointed out. "It counts. Who'd you fight?"

"Racists who made fun of my mom's accent. Rich snobs who looked down on me because my clothes came from a thrift store. Bullies who thought I was an easy target because I was small."

Shane smiled. "Did you win?"
"If I didn't have three or four of them ganging up on me."
"Do you remember how you won? What were thinking of right before the fight started?"
Shane always asked questions she'd never been asked before. She liked that about him. Talking to him was never boring. "I guess I just focused on hitting them as hard as I could. I didn't care if I got hurt, so long as I got to them. But they cared. So I won."
"And you've never fought as an adult?"
She shook her head. "I've never had to. A couple times creepy guys have tried to follow me at night, but I looked them in the eyes and yelled at them to get the fuck away from me. And they ran."
Shane nodded as if that made perfect sense. "You were in warrior mode. They could see you'd do whatever it took to win. They weren't willing to do the same, so they ran away."
"I wish you could explain that to my mom," Catalina said. "To everyone who keeps telling me to be more afraid. People always say I didn't defend myself, I was just lucky. They say that if those men had chosen to attack me, there wouldn't have been anything I could have done about it."
"They *had* chosen to attack you," Shane remarked, his expression cool and dispassionate. "Why else would they have stalked you? And you did do something about it. You won the fight without ever having to strike a blow."
He went on, "It reminds me a story I learned when I was studying karate. The two greatest swordfighters in Japan decided to duel, to see who was the best. A huge crowd gathered to watch. Everyone was sure it would be spectacular. The swordfighters walked up, squared off, and looked into each other's eyes. Then they bowed to each other and walked away. They didn't need to fight— that one look *was* the duel. There was no point even unsheathing their swords, because they already knew they were equals."
Catalina's eyes stung, just as they had when he'd told her she'd gone above and beyond the call. She already knew he thought she was brave. But everyone who knew her or saw her in action thought that. What was different about Shane was that he didn't think she was wrong or stupid or reckless to take risks. And he didn't assume that sooner or lat-

er, she'd bite off more than she could chew and pay for it with her life.

When she told him she could do something, he believed her, whether it was fighting or defending herself or carrying him. He never said, "Women can't do that" or "You're too small" or "You'll get hurt." He protected her, but like soldiers protected each other, not like a strong person protected a weak person.

Ellie treated her like that, but few other women did. And Shane was the only man she'd ever met who'd put that kind of faith in her. He probably had no idea how rare and precious that was.

She had to get him talking about something else, or she'd cry for real.

"You must love karate," she said. He'd told the story about the swordfighters with unexpected passion.

"I do. I've studied other martial arts, but that's my favorite." With a diffidence she'd never seen before, he said, "I could show you some. If you like."

"You bet!" Catalina settled in, all threat of tears evaporating in her delight at the chance to watch Shane in motion.

He moved to the middle of the floor. "Karate has some set exercises called kata. The idea is that you're fighting off imaginary opponents. I'll show you Tomari Bassai. It means 'Storming the Fortress.'"

His clear blue eyes narrowed in concentration. Then he began to move. At times he slowly stalked an unseen foe, and at times he struck too fast for the eye to follow. He turned and spun, kicking and punching and blocking, as if he was fighting off a horde of enemies that had surrounded him. He moved with the grace of a dancer and the ferocity of a warrior, every strike and turn alive with power and passion.

Finally, he came to a stop. Catalina gave a sigh of sheer pleasure.

"That was gorgeous. I wish I could do that." She stood and stretched out her leg, trying to recall one of his movements.

"Bend your other leg, too." Shane bent one leg and extended the other in front of him, with his back foot flat and only the ball of his front foot touching the floor. "It's called cat stance."

"No wonder you're good at it." She copied his stance, but could tell she wasn't getting it quite right. "What am I doing wrong?"

He stepped in close to her. She could feel the heat of his body, smell the clean scent of his sweat.

"Too much weight on your front foot. Put more on the back." His voice was husky. He was breathing harder than she'd have expected; the kata had been athletic but brief. A strand of her hair stirred with his breath.

Catalina shifted her weight, bringing herself an infinitesimal but nearly unbearable fraction closer to him. Every inch of the space between them seemed charged with tangible energy. She could have closed her eyes and traced the shape of his body in the air.

"Like this." He put his hands on her hips.

The contact went through her like an electric shock. A wave of desire broke over her. Her nerves tingled. Her nipples hardened. Her clit throbbed. The hot, slippery wetness between her thighs made it almost impossible not to squirm.

*Don't move,* she ordered herself. *He's not into you. Let him do his demo, then go take a cold shower.*

Only the palms of his hands were touching her, but she could swear she felt him breathing. Shane tugged her back and down. He was just shifting her weight, but it felt like a caress.

Catalina instinctively settled against him, unable to stop herself from seeking more contact. He was hard as steel, his erection pressing against her like a crowbar.

Startled, she twisted around, tipping her head back to look into his eyes. They blazed like blue flames, alight with a fire that could only mean one thing.

*He* does *want me,* she thought, astonished. *Why didn't he ever say so?*

"I'm losing control," he muttered, more to himself than to her. She could hear it in his voice, rough with desire and the ragged edge of passion. "I should lock myself in the bathroom."

"Don't you dare," Catalina said, and pulled his head down to hers.

He met her urgency with his own, kissing her fiercely. His mouth was hot, his stubble rough. His tongue thrust against hers, and his hands clenched on her hips. She slid her hands under his shirt, barely able to believe that he was letting her touch him. But she felt his quick inhale, in her mouth and under her palms and against her body, and knew how much he *wanted* her to touch him.

She ran her nails along his ribs, and felt him gasp again. He jerked his hips, thrusting hard against her mound. Even through two layers of jeans, the friction was electrifying. She rubbed against him, getting wetter and wetter, hotter and hotter, closer and closer to the brink. Her entire body was alight with passion that shivered through her nerves like threads of fire.

"We should get undressed," she muttered, but she couldn't bring herself to stop, even for a second. She was trembling, her muscles tense, everything in her pushing her inexorably toward her climax.

Shane held her tight. Her face was pressed against his throat; she could taste salt on his skin. "Later."

He turned his head to kiss her again, nipping at her lower lip. The slight shock of pain only added to her urgency. Her breath came in quick bursts, and her head swam. She couldn't feel her feet touching the floor. All she could sense was Shane's strong arms around her, Shane's steel-hard cock thrusting against her, and the tide of ecstasy that swept her away.

Catalina leaned against Shane, catching her breath. Her legs felt wobbly, as if they wouldn't bear her weight. Then, as she became more aware of the world, she realized that he was holding her up. And also that he was still hard as a rock.

She reached down and gripped him. He made a sound like he'd had the wind knocked out of him.

"Ready for another round?" she asked. "Or do you still want to lock yourself in the bathroom?"

"Fuck, no," Shane said.

Catalina's laugh turned into a yelp as he dropped to the floor, taking her with him. They landed with her on top. She knew he'd done that on purpose, so she wouldn't be bruised— Shane never moved clumsily or accidentally.

He lay beneath her, his chest heaving. She couldn't stand to have anything separating them, even a thin layer of cloth. Catalina sat up atop his hips and grabbed his shirt in both hands, planning to rip it off his body.

Shane caught her wrists, shaking his head. "Don't do anything to our clothes. We can't let Apex find out what we're doing."

She didn't know why it mattered, but she was hardly going to stop to ask now. She pulled his shirt off, exposing the lean muscles of his chest. He reached up to take off her shirt, then unsnap her bra.

"God, you're gorgeous." Shane cupped her breasts, then teased the nipples with his fingertips, hardening them into nubs and sending little shocks of pleasure shivering down her spine.

But good as that felt, she wanted more. She wanted skin to skin contact, everywhere, right now. Catalina peeled off her jeans and soaked panties, then dragged Shane's jeans and boxers off. His cock was hard as it could be, the head glistening and slick against her belly. She wanted to sit on it and have it fill her, immediately.

Catalina raised herself to settle down on him. Once again, Shane reached up to stop her.

"No condoms. And I can't…" He swallowed, making his Adam's apple bob. "I can't guarantee I'd pull out. Use your hands. Your mouth. Your thighs. Anything else."

Catalina remembered him saying, "I'm losing control." But he hadn't. He'd made sure she didn't get bruised. He'd stopped her from tearing his shirt. Even now, when it was probably hard to think of *anything* but getting off, he was still prioritizing her safety above his pleasure.

*What would it be like to* really *make him lose control?* Catalina wondered. *What would it be like to see that shield of his smashed to bits?*

She tapped her upper arm, feeling the matchstick sliver under the skin. "I have a birth control implant."

Catalina leaned in close, bracing her hands on his shoulders. His lithe muscles flexed and relaxed under her palms. "Shane…"

He stopped breathing, waiting for what she had to say. They looked deep into each other's eyes. He wasn't using his power, but she could sense that he *was* dangerous, and he knew it, and that was why he kept himself so cool and calm. But she knew, too, that he would never hurt her. She hoped he could see who she was, like she could see who he was. He was a dangerous man and she was a woman in love with danger. He didn't need to control himself around her.

"Bring it, Shane," she whispered. "Go wild. I can take it. I *want* it."

He drew in a deep breath, his chest expanding against hers. Next thing she knew, he was on top looking down at her, and she had her back pressed into the cool floor. She couldn't believe how fast he'd moved.

His scent of clean sweat and masculine musk filled the air. She could feel his heart pounding against her chest, speeding as fast as her own.

"I love you," he said. "That's me losing control. Not sex. Love."

For the first time, she saw the shadow of fear in his eyes. It made her heart ache at the same time that his words made her want to laugh for sheer joy. All this time, he'd been holding back because he'd thought *she* wasn't into *him?*

She cupped his face in her hands and pulled him down to her. "I love you too."

He released a long breath, warm and soft against her lips. Then he was kissing her, hot and passionate, on her mouth, her throat, her breasts. His fingers dug into her upper arms, hard enough to bruise, but she didn't care. There was a wild abandon in his kisses, in the strength of his grip, in the brightness of his eyes. It made her feel wild too. She arched her back and spread her legs, offering herself to him.

He slid into her as easily as a key into a lock. She gasped at the intensity of the sensation as she stretched to accommodate him, and at how *right* it felt to have him inside her. Her nails dug into his back as he thrust into her, rubbing against her swollen clit at every stroke. They were both panting, sweat slippery between them, hands sliding over wet skin, giving each other clumsy urgent kisses.

His thrusts grew faster, harder, as did hers. Then his teeth closed over her shoulder and bit down. The shock of pain unexpectedly pushed her over the edge. She called out Shane's name as she came, bright light expanding within her like the rising sun.

Then he was coming too, his face hidden in her hair, his teeth still locked on her shoulder. She felt him shudder and jerk against her, and then he released her and slid down to lie beside her.

Catalina managed to break the lazy stillness of the afterglow enough to raise herself on one elbow to look at Shane. He lay with his eyes closed, more relaxed than she'd ever seen him before. Even when he slept, there was a sense of watchfulness about him, as if he was ready to leap up and do battle at the slightest disturbance. Now he lay still and content, the few lines in his face smoothed out.

She wasn't going to disturb him, but he opened his eyes, rolled over, and kissed her.

"Guess my secret's out," he said.

"You're not very observant," she remarked. "I felt like I had a giant neon sign over my head that said I HAVE A CRUSH ON YOU."

"You did," Shane said casually.

Catalina blinked. "You knew? Then why was it a secret how *you* felt?"

"I didn't want Apex to know," he explained. "I was afraid that if you knew, your neon sign would light up with SHANE LOVES ME."

She punched him lightly in the arm. "Thanks a lot. I'll try to turn off the neon. But what happens if they do find out?"

The peace in Shane's eyes faded away. "They'll threaten you to control me."

Catalina had expected something much worse. "That's it? They've already tried to control *me* by threatening *you.*"

"Well, yeah, but that's me."

She punched him again, a little harder this time. "You matter too."

He seemed taken aback. "Well…"

"Shane." Catalina pulled him close, holding him tight. "You matter to me."

She felt him release his breath in a long sigh, but he didn't reply.

"Hey, strong silent type," she said. "Want to tell me what you're thinking?"

He took a deep breath, then another. When he finally spoke, she'd stopped expecting it and twitched in surprise.

"I'm scared," he admitted, then shook his head, as if in surprise at his own words. "I don't think I've said that since I was ten or something. I feel especially weird saying it now, with the power I have. But I am. The last time I was here, I… I didn't do so well."

Catalina squeezed his shoulders. "We're going to get out of here, Shane. We both rescue people for a living. We can do this. I'm not asking you to tell me about your plan— I don't want it turning up on that neon sign of mine— but you do have one, right?"

"Yeah, I do." He spoke with confidence, but Catalina wondered if she'd really persuaded him or if he just didn't want her to be scared too. "Come on, let's take a shower."

He pulled her up and put his arm around her. They went into the bathroom and wedged themselves into the tiny shower.

Shane touched Catalina's shoulder, then frowned at a smear of blood on his fingertips. "Sorry. I didn't mean to break the skin."

She glanced at the shallow bite marks. They stung a little under the hot water's spray. "Am I going to turn into a panther?"

"No!" Shane looked horrified. "God, no. I wouldn't do that to you.

I'd have to bite you when I'm a panther."

She'd figured he wouldn't do anything that he believed would harm her, no matter how out of control he felt, but she couldn't help being a bit disappointed. "You sure you don't want to? I'd be a lot more help when we escape if I could bite people's heads off."

"You'll be plenty of help without that. Can you shoot?"

"Well— I know how," Catalina said. "I went to a range a couple times with Ellie and her brother Ethan. He's a Recon Marine. I'm not a crack shot or anything."

"That should be good enough."

Catalina was desperately curious about exactly what Shane planned, beyond that he obviously intended to obtain some guns, presumably off the guards. But she didn't ask.

Instead, she lathered up her hands. "Turn around. I'll wash your back."

Shane managed to turn without either knocking her down or whacking himself on the showerhead, which was something of a miracle in the cramped cubicle. He even made the movement look graceful.

She ran her hands over his body, enjoying the simple pleasure of being able to touch him. He didn't wince when she soaped the tiny cuts her nails had left on his back and shoulders, though they had to sting as much as her bites.

"You don't need to be a panther," he said. "You've already got claws."

"Just marking my territory," she teased. "Property of Catalina Mendez. All others keep out."

"I heal fast," he reminded her, guiding her hand up to the place where he'd cut his head. She parted his sleek hair, but couldn't see or feel a scar. "You'll have to redo your keep-away signs every day or so."

He didn't sound like he'd mind. Catalina kissed one of her marks, then leaned her head against his back, blissfully happy. The warm contentment of sex still filled her, she had Shane right there in her arms, and they loved each other. She trusted him to break them out, and he trusted her to pick up a gun and fight by his side. They'd break free, and then they'd have an entire lifetime of adventures ahead of them.

It was everything she'd ever wanted, except that even in her wildest dreams, she'd failed to imagine a man as cool and sexy and brave as Shane.

*You're a bunch of losers,* she informed her imaginary boyfriends—imaginary ex-boyfriends, now. *It never even occurred to me to have any of you turn into a panther.*

Shane turned again, bent to kiss her forehead, then took the soap from her and returned the favor. She melted against him, letting him turn her this way and that to caress every inch of her body with lather-soft hands.

When they finally got out of the shower, he frowned again at the bite on her shoulder. "I shouldn't have done that. There's no way to explain it if a nurse sees it."

"Hopefully they won't make me put on a hospital gown. They didn't today."

Shane didn't look reassured. His habitual wary alertness, which had eased after they'd made love, had returned.

"Hey..." Catalina touched his arm. "You always wake up early, right?"

"Yeah."

"Let's push the beds together," she suggested. "We can move them back before Dr. Elihu shows up."

His eyes narrowed, and she knew he was weighing odds, risks, and benefits before he nodded. "Okay."

After their usual dinner of something, they moved the cots together. Catalina nestled herself against Shane and put her arms around him. His muscles were taut as strung wires, and she could guess what he was worrying about. But he held her close, making her feel loved and safe.

"Better than cats," she murmured.

"What?"

"I usually sleep with my cats," she explained. "They're nice and cozy on a cold night. But you're even cozier."

"That's definitely one of the most interesting compliments I've ever gotten from a woman," remarked Shane. "How many cats do you have?"

"Four." She waited a beat, then added, "Including you."

He chuckled, and she felt him relax.

"Don't wake me up for a shower in the morning," Catalina said sleepily. "The one we just had will do me for the day."

To her confusion, Shane again tensed beside her. "No, you should take another."

"Why?"

After a pause, he said, "I like the way your hair smells when it's wet."

She laughed in surprise. "All this time, you've been dragging me out of bed so you can *smell my hair?*"

Unabashed, Shane said, "Yes."

"You're weird." She turned her head, presenting him with her hair. "But sure. That's how much I like you, I'll let you wake me up at the crack of dawn just so you can enjoy sniffing my hair. Weird hot bodyguard."

He kissed the back of her head. "I appreciate it. Weird hot cat lady."

# CHAPTER SIX

*Catalina*

When Shane shook Catalina awake the next morning, her first thought was that they really had made love. He really did love her. It hadn't just been the sort of dream that feels great while you're having it and depresses you when you wake up and realize that it hadn't really happened.

She lazily reached up and caught his hand, bringing it to her lips. "You're real."

He bent and kissed her. "So are you. Up and at 'em."

The next thing she noticed was that the cots were already back in their usual places. She blinked up at him. "You moved the bed without waking me up?"

"You sleep like a rock." He lifted her off the cot and set her on her feet. "Go wash your hair for me."

"Why don't we shower together?"

"Can't risk it. They might show up early. If I'm outside, I won't let them open the door on you."

Catalina went and took her solo shower. When she emerged, she marched up to Shane and leaned against his chest. "Go on."

He bent and buried his face in her wet hair, taking a few deep inhales before he straightened. "Thanks. That'll keep me going for the day. Do me a favor? Listen at the door. See if you can hear them coming before they open it."

"Sure."

Shane went into the bathroom and closed the door. The room felt empty without him. Catalina spent a moment imagining Shane wet and naked, then went and listened at the door. When the clunk of the lock opening sounded right at her ear, she nearly jumped a foot in the air. Then she hastily settled down on her bed as the door swung open.

Dr. Elihu, flanked by the usual array of guards, glanced around the room and under the cots, glared at the closed shower door, then snapped his fingers at her. "Come on, Mendez."

A guard asked, "Do you want me to check the bathroom?"

The doctor turned bright red. "No, I do not!"

Catalina walked along the corridors, yawning. She'd memorized the route by now, so her mind was mostly occupied with figuring out how to conceal the bite on her shoulder if a nurse did ask her to put on a hospital gown. A sudden fit of modesty that required her to change in a bathroom? Careful handling of the gown and her shirt to make sure the nurse never saw her shoulder?

To Catalina's relief and amusement, once she got to the medical testing rooms, she was settled in front of a computer, had electrodes attached to her head, and was told to play *Grand Theft Auto 5.*

She snickered. "Seriously?"

"It's a solid test for certain reflexes, skills, and problem-solving abilities," Dr. Elihu replied condescendingly. "But I'm hardly going to stand over your shoulder and watch you giggle your way through hours of virtual mayhem."

He turned to a medical technician. "Run her for five hours. She gets a ten-minute break every half hour for the first two hours. Next three hours, run her without a break, to measure her responses under fatigue."

"Yes, doctor," said the technician.

Dr. Elihu swept out, taking three of the guards with him. The remaining three stayed in the room, their tranquilizer guns held ready.

*As if I'd try to jump three armed men,* Catalina thought. *I may be brave, but I'm not stupid.*

She turned to the screen, wondering if Shane played video games. Probably he either loved them and was a world-class player, or they bored him because he was too good at them and they weren't challenging. Though even if they did bore him, she bet he'd be glad to have them now. Even *Donkey Kong* would be preferable to one more day locked up alone.

"Play the game, Mendez," the technician ordered. She clicked a stopwatch. "Now."

Catalina began to play. She'd just blown up a bank vault when she heard a loud crack behind her. Another crack sounded as she turned around.

Shane was in the room. Two of the guards were down on the floor, and the third was swinging his gun to bear on Shane. The technician was starting to open her mouth to scream.

Catalina jumped up and clapped her hand over the woman's mouth, stifling her yell. The technician struggled with her, but Catalina held her tight. Out of the corner of her eye, she saw Shane snatch the tranquilizer gun from the last guard's hand, then punch him in the jaw. The guard dropped.

Shane turned, fast as lightning but so gracefully that it almost seemed to be in slow motion, and fired the tranquilizer gun at the technician. The woman went limp in Catalina's arms. Instinctively, Catalina caught her, then lowered her to the floor.

Then Shane and Catalina were the only ones standing, with four bodies on the floor and a bunch of bank robbers yelling on a computer screen. The entire fight had taken only seconds.

"Good work." Shane wasn't even breathing hard. He pointed to the technician. "Get into her clothes."

Catalina scrambled to strip out of her own clothing and into the technician's scrubs. The woman was taller and slimmer than her, but she squeezed into the scrubs. Shane was doing the same with the tallest guard's clothes, and also not finding them a good fit.

Catalina tried to roll up the technician's pants, but they kept flopping down. She finally took a pair of shears from a medical kit and cut them off at the ankles so they wouldn't trip her.

"Pass me that kit," Shane said.

Catalina handed it to him. He dumped out the contents, then rolled up their discarded clothes and stuck them in it.

"It might be cold outside," he explained. "I don't know where we are. I know I said I've been here before, but I meant that I've been to a base *like* this one. I'm pretty sure it's not literally the same one."

Catalina had resisted the urge to quiz him, but she couldn't stand it any more. "How in the world did you get here?"

"I told you I can sneak up on people," Shane replied, trying to wedge his feet into the guard's shoes. "I'm not invisible— people will see me if they look for me, and I show up on video— but they won't notice me if they're not looking. I walked out of the bathroom when your back was turned, lay on my cot, and pulled a blanket over myself. So long as everyone believed I was in the bathroom and didn't wonder, 'What if he's actually on the bed?' they'd just think they saw rumpled sheets. Once you all turned to go out, I followed you out the door."

"No way!" Catalina laughed, realizing how neatly he'd set it all up. "I can't believe you convinced me that you liked smelling my hair."

"I do like smelling your hair. But you had to actually believe I was in the shower. One glance anywhere else would have ruined the whole thing." Shane gave up on the guard's shoes and put his own back on. "Well, hopefully no one will notice my feet. People usually aren't very observant. Did you notice if there's any water bottles in here?"

Catalina pointed. "In that cupboard."

He stuffed as many bottles as he could fit into the kit, laid two tranquilizer guns on top, and handed her the kit. "You carry this. If I start shooting, back me up. You take the easy shots, I'll take the hard ones. Don't fire in my direction, even if it looks easy. I move pretty fast, and if I get hit by friendly fire, it's all over."

"Okay."

Shane rummaged through the unconscious guards' pockets until he found a lighter and a Swiss Army knife, which he put in his own pocket. "All right. We've got everything we need to survive."

"A lighter, a Swiss Army knife, two tranquilizer guns, a change of clothes, and four bottles of water?"

"Three tranquilizer guns." Shane indicated the holstered one at his side. He looked her over, his gaze traveling from her sneakers— the technician's shoes had been much too big for her to wear— to the badge pinned on her scrubs. Then he laid his hand on her shoulder. "Ready?"

Everything had happened so quickly, Catalina hadn't had time to register if she was afraid or not. Now that she had time, she found that she wasn't. Shane was with her, and his plan had worked spectacularly so far. Her nerves tingled with a mixture of adrenaline, excitement, trust, and love. She didn't want to be anywhere but where she was, with Shane at her side.

"Ready," she said.

# CHAPTER SEVEN

*Shane*

The cool readiness of combat filled Shane. He had no more doubt, no more fear. It didn't matter what had happened before or what might happen later. All that mattered was *now*. He wasn't a man who regretted the past or worried about losing the woman he loved. He was a predator intent on nothing but protecting his mate, defeating his enemies, and escaping his cage.

"Don't talk if anyone might be around," he said. "People who don't look at your face might recognize your voice."

"Gotcha."

He beckoned to Catalina. She followed, eagerness and excitement written all over her pretty face. She might not be a crack shot or have a poker face, but she was strong, quick-thinking, and fearless. There was no one he'd rather have at his side.

They stepped out of the medical room and into an empty corridor. He set a brisk pace, relying on his knowledge of the layout of the other base and hoping this one was similar. He glanced down each corridor they passed, until he came to a bank of elevators. He passed the security guard's badge over the sensor, and an elevator door opened.

Two guards and a doctor stepped out of the elevator.

Shane gave them a brief nod, then stepped inside the elevator. Catalina followed. Once the doors closed, he heard her breath whoosh out in a gasp.

"I can't believe they didn't recognize us," she said.

"They looked at our uniforms, not our faces." Shane hit the button with the highest number. "I think this place is mostly underground. This should take us near an exit."

The elevator doors slid open on another corridor. They once again began walking. Shane's nerves hummed with alertness. Exits were likely to be well-guarded, and they'd need to get out without an alarm being raised. He'd have to move fast, and be lucky as well.

They passed a few medical technicians, who didn't acknowledge them, and then he came to his destination, a door with six guards at the ready.

Shane walked up to it, casually holding up his badge. A guard gave it a perfunctory glance and waved him through. Shane started to step forward, unable to believe how easy it had been.

Out of the corner of his eye, he saw Catalina hold up her own badge. Another guard glanced at it, then frowned and looked back at her. "Hey— You're not Denise. What are you doing with her badge?"

Shane whipped around and slammed his elbow into the guard's jaw. The man crumpled. Before he even hit the floor, Shane drew his tranquilizer gun and fired rapidly, fanning the area. But the paralysis wasn't instantaneous, and he wasn't sure how many he'd hit. Two guards grabbed for their radios, two for their guns, and one lunged at Shane, trying to disarm him.

The radios were the biggest danger. Shane side-stepped the guard attacking him, protecting his gun-hand but taking a hard blow to the head. He wasn't close enough to either of the guards going for their radios to hit them, but he was within kicking distance of one. He roundhouse-kicked one in the head, then turned to go for the other. But Catalina was already grabbing for that guard's radio. They wrestled for it for a second, then that guard slid to the floor. Catalina had delayed the man for long enough for the dart Shane had shot him with to take effect.

A second guard dropped, paralyzed. But the guard in front of him was firing at him. Shane dropped and rolled, then kicked out from the floor, catching the man in the knee. He fell with a cry of pain that cut off as Shane kicked him in the head.

"Behind you!" Catalina gasped.

Shane rolled again, catching a quick glimpse of Catalina jumping in front of the last guard. Her back was to him, but Shane heard the soft hiss of a dart being fired. She sucked in her breath in surprise or pain. Then she dove forward, tackling the guard who had shot her. It was only a few seconds before she went limp and slid to the floor, but that was all the time Shane needed to spring to his feet and slam the guard into the wall. The man's head cracked against hard plaster, and his eyes rolled back.

Shane let him fall, forcing himself to scan the area before he did anything else. All the guards were down, unconscious or paralyzed. No one else was in sight. Only then did he kneel beside Catalina.

Other than a dart in her chest, she seemed unhurt. She was obviously paralyzed, but her eyes were open and she was breathing easily. He pulled out the dart.

"We won," he said, and kissed her cheek. "Now it's my turn to carry you."

He lifted her over his shoulders, then picked up the medical kit she'd never had time to open. The entire fight had lasted only a little longer than the one in the lab, maybe a minute. She hadn't been able to get to her gun, but she'd still stopped a guard from alerting the entire base, then taken the dart meant for Shane.

*My mate,* he thought. It amazed him as much as it had the first time he'd looked into her eyes. *My partner.*

Shane headed for the door, not knowing if he'd find scorching desert or frozen tundra or even a bustling city. Though he seriously doubted that a secret base would be in a city; it would be far too easy for any escapee to summon help with a single phone call.

He kicked the door open.

The landscape before him was green and lush, the sky overcast, the air fresh and chilly. The evergreen forest before him was backed by snow-capped mountains. Behind him, the base was disguised as a smallish government building with an entrance to an underground parking lot, and a narrow road leading out from that.

Shane ran into the forest. He undoubtedly didn't have much time before an alarm sounded— if one hadn't gone off already. Twigs snapped underfoot, but he took no care to cover his trail just yet. First, he needed to put some distance between himself and pursuit. If the way looked difficult, he took it, running between boulders and crashing through thorny bushes.

He climbed a ridge and dashed down the other side, listening for the sound of running water. Shane heard a faint rippling sound and followed it to a shallow creek. He briefly laid Catalina down, took off his shoes and tied them around his neck, then picked her up again and waded upstream, running barefoot over the smooth stones and mud that lined the bottom. The creek grew deeper and faster, then divided. Shane took the wilder route that wound through a canyon. He was in luck. The creek— now almost a river— divided again. He took a fork at random, and followed it through a series of small waterfalls, scrambling up the slippery underwater rocks, climbing with one hand and using his other to hold tight to Catalina.

He'd been hiking for hours with water up to his thighs when he heard Catalina's breathing change and felt her body jerk as she came suddenly awake.

"It's all right," he said. "I've got you."

He felt her squirm as she looked around. "Hey, we got away! Where are we?"

"It looks like the Sierra Nevada mountain range, same as their last base."

"Oh! Then you know where we are."

"Not really. The Sierra Nevadas are four hundred miles long and about seventy wide. We could be anywhere within that. I don't recognize this area at all."

She squirmed again. "Put me down. I can walk."

He shook his head. "Not yet. That shifter you met got *your* scent. They'll pick up mine too, from where we fled the base, but I'm hoping to confuse them a bit. If they can't find yours, they might think we got separated, and then they'll split up. If they do catch up with us, I'd rather deal with one at a time."

"They?" Catalina asked. "I only met one."

"There have to be two of them. At least. Shifters are either born that way, or another shifter has to bite them. Since that guy went through the ultimate predator program, he was probably bitten by some other shifter at Apex."

"Oh, right." Her silky hair brushed against his skin as she nodded. "So someone bit you, huh? Could that person have bitten the guy I met?"

"No."

"How do you know?"

He hesitated, but Catalina already knew he'd been in combat. And however unauthorized, that had sure as hell been a combat situation. "Because I killed him."

Without missing a beat, she said, "I'm sure he deserved it."

"He did."

A hard current washed around Shane's thighs, making him stagger. He held Catalina tight and dropped his center of gravity until he regained his balance. Then he set out again. His breath burned in his lungs, and his back and legs ached. Catalina was so short that despite her curves and solid build, she was no heavier than some packs he'd carried. But even with his shifter strength, it wasn't easy to run for miles with a weight across his shoulders, then trudge and climb for miles more, thigh-deep in icy water.

Thick forest pressed in on the river, the overhanging branches blocking out most of the sun. Shane's shirt was damp with sweat, but his legs were freezing. And Catalina, wearing only thin scrubs, was shivering. The water would wash away their scent, but they couldn't stay in it forever. They'd risk hypothermia.

"How are you at climbing trees?" Shane asked.

"Fantastic," she said, to his relief. "My sister used to tease me that I like cats because I am one."

"Good. I'll boost you up."

He got on to a boulder covered by only a few inches of water, with a thick branch hanging overhead. Catalina climbed on to his shoulders, then stood up. She wasn't quite tall enough to reach it, so he put his hands under her feet and slowly lifted her. She wavered, then grabbed on to the branch and held herself steady. He raised her overhead until she was able to scramble on to the branch.

"What about you?" she called down. "Turn into a panther? I could carry your clothes."

"Nah."

He handed the medical kit up to her. Shane crouched, then jumped upward. He caught the branch and pulled himself up, his muscles screaming with effort. Then he got a leg over and crouched beside

Catalina, the bark rough under his palms.

"Let's see how far we can get without touching the ground," he said.

She sat at ease, unconcerned with the height or the rushing waters beneath her, and held out a hand in invitation. "Lead on."

The forest was dense enough to make it possible for them to climb from tree to tree. There *was* something catlike about her confidence and grace as she caught and released handholds, occasionally leaping from one branch to the next.

The scent of pine and mist, her presence beside him, and her visible cheer made their journey feel more like a game than a desperate attempt at evading pursuit. His panther was content within him, enjoying the climb. And the farther they made it through the trees, the less likely it became that anyone would pick up their scent. A pursuer would have to search all along the riverbanks, think of climbing a tree, pick the exact right one to climb, *and* sniff right where they'd touched. It seemed unlikely.

To his surprise, Shane found that he was enjoying himself. He'd never before been with a woman who could keep up with him. In fact, once they were in the trees, *he* was the one trying to keep up with *her.* Though she lacked his upper-body strength, she could climb more freely than he could, able to stand on branches that wouldn't take his weight.

Finally, they came to the end of the dense woods. They were still in a forest, but a sparser one, the mossy ground broken up by boulders and stretches of bare granite. Cave-pocked hills rose up beyond the woods, and Shane could hear a river rushing somewhere below them. They'd hiked and climbed all day; the sun was sinking over the mountaintops, gilding everything in rich golden light.

Catalina nudged him. "Should we try to work our way through more forest in a different direction?"

He shook his head. "I'm pretty sure we've lost them. And it'll be night soon. We need to make a camp. We shouldn't be wandering around the woods in the dark."

"Yeah." Catalina cocked her head at the river's roar. "We might fall over a cliff. It sounds like there's one nearby."

Shane nodded. "I think this is bear territory, too."

"Bear-bears? Or werebears?"

"I wish it was werebears," Shane said. "They all know each other. All I'd have to do is say I'm a friend of Hal Brennan, and we'd get dry clothes, a home-cooked meal, a warm bed, and a ride out of here. But I meant real bears."

Catalina grinned. "I still can't get over werebears and werepanthers and were*dragons* and all being real. Well, if a real bear turns up, you can turn into a panther and scare it off, right? Or could you just stare at it and scare it off? Does your fear power work on animals?"

"Got me. I've never tried."

They climbed down from the tree, and Shane surveyed the hills. "Let me check out those caves. I'll go as a panther, just in case any of them has a bear or mountain lion inside. Yell if you need me. I won't go out of earshot."

Catalina sat down on a flat rock. "Go for it."

He undressed and handed Catalina his discarded scrubs. The wind was cold on his bare skin, but her open appreciation made him turn around slowly to give her a full view.

She applauded. "You naked against these hills… It's like a pin-up calendar."

"I'll have to make you pose for my pin-up later," he said with a grin. "Curvy Paramedics of the Woodlands."

Then he turned his focus inward.

*To stalk, to hunt, to climb into the foliage and lie in wait…*

Shane became a panther. His thick coat protected him from the cold, and his sense of smell sharpened. He sat up, sniffing the air, but smelled no other humans. There *were* bears in the area, but the scent-traces were old. None were nearby. He could scent deer and rabbits, but no large predators.

He bounded up the hillside, his paws sinking into the mossy ground, and began exploring the caves. Some he discarded for being too easily seen from outside, and others were dank and musty, the roofs covered with red-eyed bats. Some were too shallow, barely more than hollows in stone, and others were too deep, leading far into the depths of the mountain where anything might be lurking.

Then he found a cave neither too deep nor too shallow, with a dry stone floor, no bats, and an entrance concealed by a boulder and a thicket of large shrubs. No one could see it from the outside. They'd even be able to build a fire. He took a last sniff around, making sure he didn't miss anything, then ran back to Catalina.

She'd changed back into her jeans and T-shirt. She must have been freezing, but he regretted missing the sight of her naked. Catalina smiled as he approached and held out her hand, making an encouraging sound that he bet she used on her cats. He rubbed his head against her palm, and she scratched behind his ears. This time he wasn't surprised when he felt himself begin to purr, and he didn't rush to shift back, either.

A gust of wind sent dry leaves flying across the ground, and Catalina shivered. Shane shifted back. He knelt naked before her, with her hand on his head. She stroked his hair, and he turned his head to kiss her fingers. Shane heard her quick inhale as he ran his tongue over the smooth ovals of her nails and the soft pads of her fingertips. They were sticky with sharp-tasting pine sap.

Reluctantly, he pulled away to stand up, open the medical kit, and put his shirt and jeans back on. Catalina had replaced the security guard's uniform in the kit, but Shane strapped on the holster and tranquilizer gun.

He took her hand. "I found us a new home."

Shane led her up the hill, then past the boulders and shrubs and into the cave. It was dark inside, lit only by a few scarlet rays of the setting sun.

"Cozy," Catalina said, and seemed to mean it.

"Just wait." Shane gathered dry branches and twigs from beneath the shrubs, took them to the back of the cave, and lit a fire.

Catalina held her hands over it. "You're amazing. Too bad you can't snap your fingers and conjure up marshmallows to roast. Though actually— and I can't believe I'm saying this— I'm hungry enough that I'd rather have an MRE."

"I'll get us something better." He pressed a quick kiss on to the top of her head. Her hair *did* smell good, wet or dry, with a warm and spicy scent. "Hold down the fort."

He undressed, became a panther, and left the cave. Shane slipped into the nearest stretch of woods, climbed a tree, and lay on a low branch as the sunset faded to gray. It was the time of day when rabbits came out to feed. He waited until there were several nibbling away beneath him, then pounced, catching two with lightning-fast snaps of his powerful jaws. Shane picked them up and loped back to the cave, where he dropped them at Catalina's feet.

She gingerly picked them up. "Very nice. My cats bring me treats like this all the time. Only not so big. And usually they bite the heads off first."

Shane became a man and said, "Aren't you glad I can catch bigger prey than mice?"

"I'll be even more glad if you know what to do with them."

"As a matter of fact, I do."

He put his clothes back on. Then he used the Swiss Army knife to clean and dress the rabbits, while Catalina watched and made admiring remarks. Shane collected some small branches, split some to use as holders and used others to skewer the rabbits, then set up the meat to roast over the fire.

He sat down, leaning against the rough stone of the cave wall, and beckoned to Catalina. She settled down in his lap and leaned against his chest. He closed his arms around her. For the first time, it sank into him that he'd succeeded. His plan had worked. They weren't out of the woods yet, literally or metaphorically, but they weren't locked up on the base, either. He and his mate were free.

He leaned back, relaxed and content. Catalina was warm in his arms, and the fire was warm on his skin. The rabbits sizzled over the flames, and the tempting smell of grilled meat filled the cave.

When the rabbits were done, Shane pulled them off the fire. For lack of anything better, he set them on top of the medical kit. "At least it's clean."

"You always make me such fancy gourmet meals," Catalina said, then ate a chunk of meat. "Oh, hey, this is actually really good. Try it."

She pulled off another chunk and held it to his lips. He opened his mouth, taking the bite of rabbit from her fingers. It *was* good, tender and juicy. His hunger awakened. They devoured the rabbits, nibbling the bones free of every scrap of meat, and washed them down with bottled water.

"Just pretend there's wine and candles," said Shane.

"You can treat me to the real thing when we get back home." Catalina snuggled back into him. "How long do you think that'll take, by the way?"

He shrugged. "Well, there's a base with employees, and a paved road. We can't be *that* far from civilization. If we head west, eventually we'll get out of the mountains. Could be a day, could be a week."

"I'll think of it as a hiking trip." She yawned so widely that he heard her jaw pop. Shane wasn't surprised. He too was tired from fighting and hiking and climbing, not to mention the built-up tension of his capture and imprisonment.

He thought about keeping watch or having them trade off watches. But they'd be more conspicuous and easily scented if they left the cave than if they stayed in it. And if all they could do was listen, he might as well sleep. He'd wake up at the slightest noise.

"Let's get some rest," Shane said.

They spread out their scrubs on the floor, then lay on top of them, still in their clothes. She fit so easily into his arms, her head pillowed on his shoulder as if they'd been made to fit together. He inhaled the scent of her hair and listened to her breathing deepen as she drifted off.

But despite his weariness, even despite having his mate in his arms, sleep eluded him. Shane lay awake, unable to move without waking Catalina and unable to shut off his restless thoughts. The peace he'd felt earlier slipped away, leaving him edgy and wired.

*You should be* more *relaxed, not less,* he told himself. *You escaped. You won. Soon you and Catalina will be safe and home.*

And then…

Catalina turned in her sleep, nestling even closer to him. She trusted him so completely. Would that change when— if— she learned the truth about him?

*You're free now,* a voice whispered within him. *Who's going to tell her? She never needs to know.*

That voice didn't belong to his panther. It was pure Shane— the worst part of Shane.

*I can't lie to my mate,* he told the devil on his shoulder. *I'll tell her everything… once we're out of the woods. If I tell her now, she might not want to stick with me, and she needs me to bring her safely home.*

The vow of honesty brought him no more peace than the impulse to lie. He lay awake for what felt like hours, thinking of every wrong thing he'd ever done and picturing Catalina turning her back on him and walking away. Forever. Finally he succumbed to sheer exhaustion, and slept.

***

*"Shane…" Justin's grip was weak in Shane's hand, his fingers cold. His skin was drained of color. It made his copper hair look brighter than ever.*

*Shane held his hand tight. "Hold on, Red. You're going to be all right."*

*"I can't… breathe." Justin's voice was not only choked but frightened. He parachuted into combat with a grin and a joke. Nothing scared him.*

*Hands gripped Shane's shoulders, trying to pull him away from Justin. Shane hung on. If he let go, Justin would die.*

*Then he wasn't holding Justin any more, but Catalina. Her brown skin had gone ashen. She too looked frightened.*

*"Shane…" she whispered. "I can't…"*

"Shane?"

He sat bolt upright, gasping, his heart pounding. Instinctively, he snatched for a weapon, but his fingers closed on empty air.

The fire had burned low, but cast a flickering light. Catalina was sitting up, beside him but not touching him. It was still dark outside.

His hair was damp with sweat, his throat raw, his muscles painfully tense. He didn't trust himself to speak.

*Catalina's fine,* he told himself. *She hasn't done the process. It's not too late. You saved her.*

But he hadn't saved Justin. And they weren't yet out of the woods. And she still didn't know who she was traveling with.

"What were you dreaming about?" Catalina asked.

*Tell her,* hissed his panther, startling him.

"I don't remember," Shane said, much too late to be convincing.

"Bullshit," she said crisply. "Don't lie to me."

"I…" Shane fished for something to say that wouldn't be a lie. "If I tell you now, it might put you in danger."

"I call bullshit on that, too."

He was too taken aback to argue. No one flat-out contradicted him like that, unless you counted his panther.

His panther gave a huff of approval. *He* agreed with Catalina.

*You would,* thought Shane. *You don't think we did anything to be ashamed of.*

Catalina went on, "I don't mind your little white lies about the shower. I knew you weren't telling me everything, but you had a reason for that and I agreed to it. But I don't agree to being lied to now. If it's too painful to talk about, just say so."

He sat in silence, his arms wrapped around his chest. Despite the fire, he felt chilled. But Catalina was right. What sort of mate could he be to her if he couldn't tell her the truth?

"It is too painful to talk about," he said at last. "But I will anyway. I dreamed of my best friend dying. He said he couldn't breathe, and then he passed out and died. That really happened. And then I dreamed that it was you. It was you, dying in my arms."

"I'm so sorry, Shane." Catalina reached out to put her arm around his shoulders.

The chill went right down to his bones as he raised his hand, warding her off. "Don't touch me."

"Are you sure? You're shivering."

"I have to tell you something first. You should know before you touch me again. I wasn't just imprisoned by Apex. I worked for them. I was an assassin."

She didn't recoil in horror. She didn't walk out. She didn't even look surprised. "I know."

He stared at her, baffled. "You know? Did Dr. Elihu tell you?"

"He didn't have to. I figured it out." With a touch of impatience, she said, "You told me yourself, Apex is a black ops agency. What else would they want you for?"

"Black ops just means illegal and secret. I could've been a spy or a saboteur or— or anything." Then his thoughts caught up to his mouth. "You knew all along? But—" He couldn't quite bring himself to say, *"But you said you loved me."*

"Shane, you were kidnapped. This wasn't something you chose to do. How could I hold it against you?" Catalina's face, which gave away everything she felt, showed nothing but honesty and acceptance and touch of sadness— sadness for *him*.

He swallowed, unable to speak. Deep in his heart, he'd always believed that their relationship was real but temporary— that once Catalina knew what he'd done, what he *was*, she'd leave him. But she'd known all along, and she hadn't gone anywhere.

She hadn't left him, and she didn't fear him. She was sitting right there, one hand raised slightly as if she still wanted to put her arms around him. But he'd told her not to touch him.

He reached out to her, catching her hand and tugging her toward him. Catalina slid over without a second's hesitation, pressing her side against his and wrapping her arms around him. She picked up his hands and rubbed them. "You're freezing."

His hands tingled as blood began to rush back into them. He leaned his head on her shoulder and breathed in the scent of her hair. It reminded him of cinnamon and ginger, sensual yet familiar and comforting.

A tight knot of pain and grief inside his chest began to loosen, allowing him to speak again. "There's more. I wasn't the only person Apex tried to turn into an ultimate predator. I'm supposed to rescue people, but I couldn't save any of them. Everyone died but me."

"That's terrible, but that wasn't your fault, either." Her arms tightened around him. "I haven't saved everyone I wanted to save, either. I've had people die in my arms, too. They were patients, not friends, but still."

Shane felt as raw and exposed as if he'd been sunburned all over. The question he wanted to ask would expose him even more, but he had to ask. "How do you live with it?"

"I remember everyone I did save." Catalina turned to press her lips into his cheek. "You've saved people, too. That's what PJs and bodyguards do. And you saved me."

The tangle of old hurt knotted around his heart slowly unraveled, letting him breathe freely. He *had* saved people. One of them was right there with him, alive and warm, holding him in her arms. She knew what he'd done and what he'd failed to do, and she loved him anyway. She was a fighter, like him. And like him, she hadn't always won.

Why had he been so caught up in thinking she could never understand or trust him if he told her the truth? He'd been the one who hadn't understood or trusted her.

"I can tell you everything," he offered. "The entire story, if you're not too tired. I've never told it to anybody. But I'd like you to know."

"I'm not tired," Catalina replied. "I'm a night owl— I'm completely awake. And of course I want to know your story. I love you."

# CHAPTER EIGHT

## *Shane's Story*

I went through PJ training with a guy named Justin Kovac. The Pipeline is one of the longest special ops training courses— it takes nearly two years— and less than a quarter of everyone who starts makes it through. By the time we were done, we might as well have been brothers. I was pretty intense back then— I guess that hasn't changed— but Justin was more easygoing. He used to play pranks, tell jokes, get me to lighten up.

We all had nicknames based on how we looked or our names or dumb stuff we did in training. Justin had green eyes and hair the color of a new penny. Not exactly a redhead, but close enough to get him nicknamed Red. I got named after an old cowboy movie, *Shane*. At the end Shane leaves town, while this kid yells after him, "Come back, Shane! Come back!" So they called me Comeback.

We were PJs for ten years. Sometimes we were on the same team, sometimes not, but we always kept in touch. There were other guys I was friends with, and Justin was more outgoing than me so he had buddies everywhere. But I was closest to him. Like you and Ellie, I think.

I already told you Apex captured me while I was on a mission overseas. What I didn't tell you is that they got everyone who went on that mission. Not just the PJ team. They also kidnapped the helicopter crew that was transporting us. Six men, two women— the helo pilot and one of the door gunners were female. I hadn't met the helo crew before, but I knew the other two PJs, Armando and Mason. We weren't best friends, but they were good guys. The third PJ was Justin.

I can't get into the details of the mission. It's probably still classified. So I won't say exactly how we were all captured. I'm sure Apex meant to take us all alive and unharmed. But we were already in a combat situation— they took advantage of that, used it to cover up what they were doing— but while the Apex guys were shooting at us with tranquilizer rifles, the enemy was using actual bullets. Justin took a round to the chest. I was trying to stop him from bleeding to death when I got nailed by a tranquilizer dart and passed out.

When we woke up, we were on a base pretty similar to the one you and I escaped from. Dr. Elihu was there, too. He designed the ultimate predator process. He bragged about it to us— he was proud. Said it was completely revolutionary and he'd win the Nobel if it was ever declassified. At first we didn't believe him. But he had us watch while his buddy, this guy named Blackburn, turned into a leopard. Then we believed it.

A helo pilot and co-pilot, two helo door gunners, and four PJs— you'd think we could escape from anywhere. But Justin couldn't travel and we couldn't leave him. They were keeping us all together, in a sort of high-security hospital barracks. He was getting good medical care, but he wasn't going anywhere anytime soon. He couldn't even sit up in bed. So we decided to wait till he'd recovered, and then we'd all make a break for it.

They took Elizabeth, one of the door gunners, first. Blackburn bit her, and then she could turn into a leopard. Even though we were pissed at being kidnapped, we all thought that was pretty cool. Elizabeth sure did. Then they put her through the ultimate predator process. And she died.

At first we didn't realize just how risky ultimate predator was. Dr. Elihu made out like Elizabeth dying was some kind of freak accident. Then he chose Neil, the co-pilot. It went down exactly the same as it had with Elizabeth: Neil became a leopard, and that went fine. Then they took him for the process, and he didn't make it.

We realized that we couldn't wait for Justin to get better. By then the rest of us would be dead. So we decided to stage an uprising once the next guy got bitten. That hadn't hurt Elizabeth or Neil, and we figured we could use a leopard shifter on our side. We hoped to get to a phone or radio and call for help. Our backup plan was that one of the PJs would try to sneak out while the rest of us were fighting. I wouldn't leave Justin, so we decided that Armando would try to get out, or Mason would try if Armando was the one who became a leopard.

But it turned out that just getting bitten could kill people. Blackburn bit Mason, but he didn't become a shifter. He just died.

Then it was down to five of us. We went ahead with our plan anyway, but we never got near a phone, and Armando didn't make it out. All that happened was that we did some damage before we all got tranquilized. After that we were guarded much more closely. They chained up everyone who was going to get bitten, so they couldn't do anything once they became a shifter. Armando and Rosa and Tyrone survived getting bitten, but not ultimate predator.

Finally Justin and I were the last ones left. He was doing better by then— he could get out of bed and walk around the room— but it would be weeks before he was up to running or fighting. He told me to forget about him and escape by myself. But there was no way I'd leave him there, wounded and imprisoned and alone.

Blackburn came in to bite Justin, and I did my best to kill him. He was a shifter, way stronger than I was then, but I was a better fighter. I might've had a chance, except for those fucking tranquilizer guns. I got knocked out, and when I woke up, Justin had been bitten.

His wound was nearly healed, and he was much stronger than he'd been just a few hours before. Nobody had told us that shifters had healing powers. Those bastards at Apex had deliberately let Justin suffer instead of having Blackburn bite him right away, just to make it harder for the rest of us to escape.

Apex waited a couple days, until Justin was completely recovered. They drugged us both so we couldn't fight, and put him through the process. It had gone wrong for the others right away, but Justin seemed fine. Dr. Elihu was all excited. And I— I was sure he'd make it.

Then he collapsed. Everything happened so fast after that. One second he was talking to me, the next second he'd stopped breathing. I started doing CPR, but Dr. Elihu and his medical team tried to take him away from me. I knew they were going to try to resuscitate him, but I wouldn't let go of him. I *couldn't.* So I got tranquilized again.

When I woke up, he was gone.

I didn't fight when Blackburn came for me. With no one left to protect, I didn't care if I lived or died. But once he bit me, I felt differently.

It's hard to explain if you're not a shifter. Even if you were born a shifter, I think it's different than if you were made into one. My panther's me. But he's me with a voice and body and instincts that are different from me, Shane. He's the part of me that's pure predator— that doesn't care about anything but the hunt and the kill and survival. *He* sure cared whether he lived or died.

By the time they put me through the process, my panther had changed how I felt. I was absolutely determined to live and escape. My panther didn't like being trapped any more than I did.

And I survived.

I have no idea why I was the only one. Everyone else had been just as determined to live as I was. But it had gone a little differently for me from the beginning. Blackburn was a leopard, and the others he bit became leopards. Technically, I am too. A panther isn't a different species, it's just a black leopard or black jaguar. But I looked different.

That probably had nothing to do with why I survived, though. Justin's leopard looked different, too, and it didn't save him. His fur was white instead of yellow. When I met Fiona at Protection, Inc., I realized that he'd been a snow leopard, like her.

Once I'd gotten through the process, I found out that I could make people not notice me. I don't think anyone at Apex was expecting that. I demonstrated my fear power, so they'd think they knew what my power was— and that it was the only power I had. I gave them a couple days to let down their guard, and then I walked out without anyone noticing. I stole one of their cars and a couple of their wallets, and took off.

I wish now that I'd gone back to my Air Force base. I thought of it. But I didn't know if Apex was a government agency or what. If they were, I might just be delivering myself straight back to them. And I was afraid that if I contacted anyone I knew, I'd put them in danger.

Once I could get online, I looked myself up. Apex had put a story out that we'd all been killed in action when our helo had gone down over the ocean, so there were no bodies. That made me really reluctant to contact anyone in the government— that was a hell of a cover-up.

Apex had to be powerful. Anyone I talked to might just turn me over to them.

So I ran halfway across the country, then hid out in a big city. I figured I could lose myself there for a while and think things over. But I didn't know as much about hiding my tracks then. And I didn't know a clock was ticking.

I was free for about a week, and then I got sick. I thought it was the flu. The symptoms were a pretty good match— weakness and fatigue, fever and chills, pain in my bones and joints. At first I wasn't worried. I'm a PJ, right? I'm strong. I figured I'd just hole up where I was, in this dirtbag motel I'd checked into under a fake name, and drink a lot of water.

But I got a lot worse, really fast. By the next morning, I could barely stand up. Then I thought maybe I had pneumonia. I was worried Apex would find me if I went to an ER, so I decided to take a taxi to a clinic. I figured I could get antibiotics without having to check myself in anywhere. But I didn't even make it out the front door of the motel. I passed out in the lobby, and someone called 911.

I woke up in the ICU. The doctors told me my heart was failing. I was young and I looked strong, but I was dying and they couldn't figure out why. They wanted to know my complete medical history and if I'd traveled abroad recently. I tried to stick to my cover story, but it's hard to lie well when you're that sick.

By then I'd guessed that what was really going on was the ultimate predator process catching up to me. I figured it was even money whether or not I'd die of that before Apex found me.

It turned out that Apex was already hot on my trail. They'd tracked me down to the city I was in, and they'd already started contacting hospitals asking for a man of my description with my symptoms. They said I had a rare virus and needed to be quarantined. I was in the hospital for less than a day before Apex found me and had me medevaced back to the base.

So I ended up right back where I started. That was when Dr. Elihu explained to me that I needed regular treatments that I could only get from Apex, or the process would kill me after all.

I didn't want to die. I especially didn't want to die like that, slowly in a hospital bed. I'd always wanted to die in combat, on my feet. I decided to play along, do as I was told, and figure out how to replicate the treatment so I could get away later.

But the only way I could deal with being an assassin was to let my panther take over. *He* was fine with lying in wait to kill people. So I let myself just become the predator.

In a way, it felt good. It was like being in combat or practicing martial arts. There was nothing but *doing*. I didn't plan anything past the end of a mission. I didn't grieve. I didn't think about the past or future. I lost track of time. A year went by, and it barely felt like a month.

Then they sent me to kill an arms dealer. He was my age and had hair the color of a new penny. He was a bad guy, for sure— none of the people Apex sent me after were innocent— so I went ahead and took him out. But it made me think of Justin. Apex had killed him, and I'd never paid them back for that. And it reminded me of who I used to be.

I'd never figured out what the treatment was. And if I hadn't in a year, I never would. But I was tired of being nothing but a predator. I wanted to be Shane again, even if it cost me my life.

I went back to the base and did the treatment, one last time. Once I was done, I broke into the base commander's office and killed him. Then I went looking for Dr. Elihu. But the alarm got raised before I found him. I was near an exit, so I had to make a decision. I could either keep fighting and eventually get tranquilized, or run.

I shifted and took off into the forest. Blackburn went after me, as a leopard. He caught up with me and we fought. Physically, we were a pretty even match. But he was fighting me because it was his job, and I was fighting him to pay him back for what he did to Justin and the other PJs and the helo crew. I'd never wanted anything more in my life than I wanted to kill him. And I did.

I was clawed and bitten all over, but I waded through streams so I wouldn't leave a trail of blood. I went deeper and deeper into the wilderness until I was sure I'd lost any pursuit. I hunkered down for a couple days to let my wounds heal, and then I headed out again.

I found a backpack hidden under a rock. It had clothes and boots in it. The scent was old— whoever it belonged to hadn't touched it in years. So I took it. The clothes were too big for me, but they more or less fit. Then I kept hiking as a man. I've always loved the wilderness. It seemed like a good way to spend the rest of my life.

After a week or so, I started getting sick. It was exactly like when I'd escaped the first time, so I knew my time was up. I kept walking till I collapsed and couldn't get up again. I was in a glen by a stream, beneath a huge maple tree turning yellow and red. I lay where I'd fallen, and I watched the water flowing and the leaves drifting down until I passed out.

I was way out in the middle of nowhere. It never occurred to me that anyone would find me. But someone did. I was drifting in and out of consciousness, but I woke up when someone put their hand on my forehead.

This huge guy was kneeling beside me, looking concerned. He said, "Can you talk to me? My name's Hal Brennan. What's yours?"

I sure wasn't going to tell him. I said, "Get your hands off me."

Hal took his hand off my forehead, but he didn't go away.

"Are you lost?" he asked. "You have a fever."

I knew he meant well, but I was pissed off at him. I'd done terrible things to survive, and I was dying anyway so it had all been for nothing. I hadn't saved anyone, not even myself. I hadn't gotten the chance to be killed in action, doing something useful. And now I couldn't even die in peace without this big lunk bothering me.

I said, "I'm fine. I'm just taking a nap."

"I don't think so," he said. "Can you even sit up?"

I figured that would get rid of him, so I tried. I managed to lever myself up halfway, and then I collapsed. Hal caught me and lowered me down.

"You need to go to a hospital," Hal said.

"I don't want a hospital," I said. "Take off."

Hal didn't move. He said, "Buddy, you're sick. You're burning up, and you're not thinking straight. If you don't get medical care, you could be in big trouble."

He bent down like he was going to try to lift me. I didn't have the strength to fight, so I hit him with fear. He rocked back a bit, then held his ground and *growled* at me. I'd never heard anything like it.

We stared at each other for a moment. Then he relaxed and said, "You must be a shifter. I am too. I'm a bear."

I believed him. Who would even mention shifters if they weren't one? And something about him made me trust him, at least a little bit.

I said, "I'm a panther."

Hal took a second look at me and chuckled. "Hey, you found one of my emergency clothes stashes! But you're welcome to it. I'm sure you needed it more than I did."

He put his hand on my shoulder and said, "Don't worry about the hospital. I know a doctor who's a shifter herself. She'll know how to treat you and she won't tell a soul."

"There's nothing anyone can do for me," I said.

He frowned and said, "Are you sure? What's the matter with you?"

"I don't know," I said. "I was kidnapped and experimented on. I just know that I'm dying. I want to die here, in the woods, not with a tube down my throat in some white room with no windows."

Hal looked around, then he touched a red maple leaf lying on the moss. It looked tiny next to his hand. He said, "I get it. I'd want the same thing, if it was my time. But you shouldn't give up the fight just yet. How about this. I'll take you to Dr. Bedford. If she can't help you, I'll bring you back."

I wanted to make sure he meant it, so I asked him, "You promise that you'll bring me back and leave me here?"

"No," Hal said. "I'll bring you back, and then I'll stay with you until you go."

Up till then, I *had* given up. I felt like I'd failed everyone— Justin, Armando, Mason, the helo crew, the Air Force, myself. But here was this stranger telling me he'd stay with me so I wouldn't have to die alone. It was the sort of thing any airman would do for another. It made me feel like I was part of something again.

I still didn't think I was going to make it. But I decided to keep fighting anyway.

I told him, "It's a deal. And my name's Shane Garrity."

Hal carried me through some pretty rough terrain, for hours, to a doctor in the little town he's from.

He was afraid I'd die if I passed out again, so he talked to me to keep me awake. He told me all about himself— Ellie probably told you he used to be a Navy SEAL— and about Protection, Inc. He said his team were all shifters who didn't fit in where they'd come from, but they fit with each other. I couldn't talk much— by the time we got to town, I was having a lot of trouble breathing— but I did manage to tell him that I was a PJ and I used to rescue guys like him. He said he was glad to have the chance to return the favor.

Hal brought me to Dr. Bedford's office. She was a bear shifter too, a black woman with wire-rimmed glasses and hair in cornrows.

Dr. Bedford examined me. She said it looked like my body was rejecting the ultimate predator process, like I'd been given a transfusion of the wrong blood type. I'd figured that much out. She told me I had a choice. She could keep me alive as long as possible, and hope that at some point, my shifter healing would kick in and either reverse the process or help my body adapt to it. But she'd have to put me on life support, which was exactly what I didn't want. Or Hal could take me back to the forest and stay with me until I died.

By then I felt like Hal was a friend. I couldn't do that to him. And it didn't feel right to just give up and die. I'd never have gotten through the Pipeline if I was the kind of person who quit when things got tough. So I asked her to go ahead and put me on a ventilator.

Once she did that, I'd have a tube down my throat and I wouldn't be able to talk. Hal asked me if there was anyone I wanted to call first, to come stay with me. I said no. So he said he'd stay with me. I told him he'd already gone above and beyond the call, and he didn't need to do anything more. He said I wouldn't have left him if he'd been wounded in action, and he wasn't going to leave me. And that was that.

Being on life support was even worse than I'd imagined. My panther hated the machines and tubes and needles, and I was too weak to keep him from taking over and too out of it to explain that everything was there to help us. I kept waking up thinking I was back at Apex, and then I'd try to tear everything out. But Hal didn't let me do anything to hurt myself. Sometimes he had to hold me down until Dr. Bedford could give me a sedative, but sometimes he just talked to me until I calmed down.

One time I came to feeling really bad. Dr. Bedford told me later that my heart had stopped. She and Hal had traded off doing CPR for forty minutes, and they'd been about ready to give up. But all I knew then was that my chest hurt and I felt like I was dying. Dr. Bedford was giving me a shot and looking worried, and Hal was slapping my face. Not hard, but enough to wake me up.

Once I opened my eyes, Hal grabbed my hand and said, "Stay with me, Shane."

I was so far gone, I didn't even recognize him. I thought he was Justin and I tried to ask him why he'd dyed his hair brown. But something was stuck in my throat, and I couldn't speak.

He said, "Don't try to talk. Just listen. Your panther's stronger than you are. You have to let him fight for you now. Wake him up, and tell him to fight for his life."

My head cleared a little, and I remembered who he was. I trusted that he knew what he was talking about. And I didn't want to be the sort of person who gave up. I never had been, before. If I gave up now, that would prove that Apex really had broken me.

Hal wasn't giving up either. He yelled at me, "Wake up your panther, Shane! Tell him to fight!"

I looked into myself until I found my panther. He didn't look in any better shape than I was, but I woke him up and told him he had to fight for both of us.

At first he didn't seem to care. That scared me. He's my survival instinct, the part of me that wants to live no matter what. If my panther didn't care if he lived or died, I was probably too far gone to make it.

In real life, I couldn't speak or stand. But inside my mind, I could do anything. All it took was willpower. So I dragged my panther to his feet and slapped his face until he opened his yellow eyes and snarled at me.

"Your turn," I said. "Fight for both of us. Fight for our lives!"

That took all my strength. Once I'd done it, I passed out.

Next time I woke up, I was feeling better. I was still on an IV and oxygen and a heart monitor, but I was off the ventilator. And if that hadn't been enough to tell me I'd turned the corner, Hal wasn't talking to me or pinning me down. He was in a chair beside my bed, fast asleep with a book in his lap.

I'd been on life support for a week. But once I was breathing on my own, I got better fast.

I never did tell Hal the whole story of what happened to me. You know more now than he does. But I told him enough that he knew that I couldn't go back to my old life. So he offered me a job.

I wasn't sure about working on a team again. I wasn't sure about anything any more. But I trusted Hal. He'd gone above and beyond for me when all he knew about me was that I was a shifter and a PJ. And he'd already been trying to rescue me when all he knew was that I was sick and I needed help. I figured his team had to be all right. Also, I had no money, and I wanted to pay back Dr. Bedford.

So I joined Protection, Inc. Rafa, Fiona, Destiny, and Nick were already on the team. Lucas joined after I did. At first I felt like the odd man out, but after a while I realized that Hal hadn't been kidding when he'd told me all of them were odd men out. Even him. But we did all fit together. Even me.

That was a year ago. I've been using a fake last name, and I don't take assignments where I could end up on the news. I figured Apex had to think I was dead, and so long as I didn't bring myself to their attention, they'd never learn otherwise. But either I slipped up or they got lucky.

You know the rest.

# CHAPTER NINE

*Shane*

When Shane had begun his story, he hadn't even been sure he could get through it. But it was easier to tell than he'd expected, especially with Catalina's arms around him. She never let go and she never flinched, no matter what he'd confessed. By the end of it, he was even smiling a little, remembering what a jackass he'd been to Hal and how completely Hal had ignored Shane's attempts to get rid of him.

Catalina also seemed to be recalling the same part. "You really don't like being the person who gets rescued, instead of being the rescuer."

"I don't," Shane admitted. "But I appreciate it anyway. I'm glad Hal didn't leave me. And now that you're safe, I'm glad you didn't, either."

"I'm glad, too." Catalina stroked his hair until he would have purred if he could. Then she said, "None of what you told me makes me feel differently about you. You did your best. If it had been me, I probably would have done basically the same things. Except that I might not have run the second time. I don't mind risking my life, but I don't know if I could bring myself to do something that I *knew* would kill me."

"I didn't know that about myself, either," Shane replied. "I don't think you can know until you actually have to make that choice."

"I hope I never do."

With all his heart, Shane said, "I hope so, too."

Her hand moved downward, from his hair to his shoulder. She slipped her hand under his collar and squeezed the muscle, her strong fingers digging in until it softened under her touch. Then she moved on to his other shoulder. He relaxed into her massage, his tension slipping away. He felt as if a weight he'd been carrying for years, like a rucksack so heavy that the straps had worn grooves into his shoulders, had been lifted off his back.

*I should tell Hal the whole story,* he thought. *I should tell Fiona.*

*I should tell all of them. They're my brothers and sisters. They'll understand.*

Catalina pressed a kiss into the nape of his neck. He could still feel it after she lifted her head, hot as the desert sun. Heat ran down his spine and through his veins, but in a slow burn rather than the searing, desperate passion of the night before.

He turned to kiss Catalina, running his fingers through her silky hair. It flowed against his skin like water, cool and smooth and scented like her. She put her hands under his shirt, tracing his ribs and then sliding up his back. It was everything he could ever want, and not nearly enough. That sweet caress reminded him of how long it had been since he'd touched anyone, except for fighting or sparring or brief necessity. He used to love touching and being touched, the simple pleasure of skin on skin.

"Last night was the first time I'd had sex in nearly three years," Shane said.

Catalina's hands paused briefly, then she resumed caressing him. "Really?"

"First most-of-a-year, I didn't have a girlfriend and I was overseas a lot. Second year, I was with Apex. Third year…" He broke off, feeling himself tensing up, and concentrated on the warmth of her body against his. "I didn't want to get close to anyone. Not even for a night. Especially not for a night. I didn't want anyone to say, 'Shane, what were you dreaming about?'"

Catalina kissed him, then said seriously, "Next time, would you rather I didn't ask?"

He shook his head. "You can ask. I've spent too long hiding in the shadows. Feel free to drag me out."

"Like a cat lurking under a bed," she said with a smile. "I don't need to drag you out— I'll just open a can, and you'll come running."

Shane smiled, relaxing again. "Or open an MRE."

"I've got something even more tempting for you." Catalina settled down in his lap, rocking her hips into his.

He was already hard as a rock, but that made him *ache* with desire. All he wanted was to bury himself in her wet heat, and feel her tight walls gripping him until he exploded inside her. But he didn't recklessly give in to impulses. He controlled them. They didn't control him. First, he had to remember if there was anything else he should do, anything he should check, any chance—

"Lie down." Catalina put her palm on his chest and pushed him down until he lay on his back and she was perched atop him. She pulled off his shirt, then ran her hands over his shoulders. Her fingers barely dented his taut muscles. "You're so tense. What are you thinking?"

"I'm trying to figure out if this is going to distract me so much that I won't hear if someone sneaks up on us," he admitted.

"Shane, you'd hear someone even if you were asleep, right? I assume you wouldn't have slept, otherwise."

She knew him so well. He liked the intimacy of it, but it felt risky, too. "You sitting on my cock is way more distracting than being asleep."

Catalina grinned and adjusted her seat. That was even more distracting. "Do you really think there's any chance whatsoever that you wouldn't hear footsteps? That you wouldn't hear someone shoving through all those bushes to get to the cave? Or that I wouldn't, even if someone managed to sneak up while you were busy having a three-minute orgasm?"

Shane couldn't help chuckling. "No."

"Then relax." Her voice lowered to a purr. She took off her shirt and bra, exposing her plump breasts and luscious brown nipples. "Lie back and let me do the work."

He reached up, caressing that soft flesh. Her scent, her warmth, the pressure of her mound against his cock, her throaty tones as she said, "let me do the work"— all of it made his mind reel. He stopped trying to think, let go of even the smallest part of his mind that consciously kept watch, and abandoned himself to pure sensation.

She pulled off his jeans, then wriggled out of her own. Every movement made her breasts quiver, and her hair fell across her face like black satin. Her scent was even stronger with her jeans off, tangy and sweet and womanly.

When she raised herself over him, a drop of liquid fell on to his cock, tracing a warm line down his exquisitely sensitive skin. He groaned and thrust up to meet her.

Catalina rocked back, allowing her wet folds to slide along his cock without letting him penetrate her. The sensation was shocking, ecstatic, and maddening. She rubbed herself over him, marking him with her scent, her lips curled in teasing pleasure. He heard himself gasping, his pulse thundering in his ears. He couldn't think of anything but sinking himself inside her.

Then she leaned forward, bracing her palms on his shoulders, and slid down to surround him. An electric jolt of pleasure flashed through him, making him groan aloud. She was hot and wet and tight inside. Just being inside her was nearly enough to make him come then and there.

Catalina rode him hard, matching his thrusts, her hands clenched hard on his shoulders. She was panting, her lips parted, her skin glowing with a light mist of sweat. She'd never been more beautiful, wrapped up in her own pleasure. Shane held her wrists, keeping her steady, giving himself something to hold on to lest he be completely swept away.

He felt as well as saw her come, her walls clenching and pulsing around him as she threw back her head and gasped. Her eyes were closed, her black eyelashes fluttering, her lovely face transfigured with the intensity of her orgasm. Shane wanted to stay in that moment forever, gripped in her wet heat, seeing the pleasure he was giving her. But his body pushed him onward, thrusting harder and faster, until the last thread of his control snapped and he shattered into white-hot ecstasy.

Shane slowly returned to the world: the sound of Catalina's breathing, her body warm beside his, her arm across his chest and her fingers clasping his, the crackle of the fire, the scent of smoke and sex. He lay still and relaxed, sensing rather than thinking, wanting nothing more than the present moment. Gradually, he began to drift into sleep.

A rustle and snap jarred Shane out of his pleasant doze. He sprang to his feet, instantly on full alert, all senses attuned for danger.

Catalina grabbed for the medical kit, opening it and yanking out a pair of tranquilizer guns.

Another rustle and snap, this one closer. Some heavy creature was approaching, crunching leaves and twigs beneath its feet. Shane took one of the guns from Catalina, crept to the entrance of the cave, and peered out.

The darkness outside had lightened to the blue dimness of pre-dawn. In that faint light, he saw an enormous grizzly bear stalking toward the cave.

"Bear," Shane whispered. He handed the gun back to Catalina without taking his eyes off the grizzly. "It probably smelled the rabbits. I don't think darts will stop it— I'll scare it off."

He stepped out of the cave, confronting the bear in his human form. He didn't know if his fear power worked when he was a panther— the big cat was perfectly capable of terrifying humans without any special assistance— and ever since Catalina had suggested using it on animals, he'd been curious whether that would work.

The bear stopped, swinging its great head toward him. Shane found the part of him that was pure predator, that felt no fear or hesitation, that lived for nothing but the kill. Then he looked into the bear's shiny black eyes.

The grizzly looked right back at him. Shane had wondered if it was a shifter from Apex, but there was no human intelligence in its gaze. It was a wild animal, nothing more. And it sure didn't seem scared. If anything, he seemed to have annoyed it. The bear growled, then began approaching faster.

*Bears are supposed to be scared of humans,* Shane recalled from years of hiking in the woods. *Any humans, not just me. Stand tall, wave your arms to make yourself look bigger, and yell. They'll run away.*

He waved his arms and yelled. "Go away! Get lost!"

The grizzly bear growled again, and charged.

Shane shifted faster than he ever had before, leaping to the side the instant the change was complete. His panther was quick, but so was the bear. The grizzly caught him in mid-leap, bowling him over with its superior weight and sending him rolling head over tail down the hillside.

Shane scrambled to his feet, startled but unhurt. The grizzly swung around, its attention now fixed on Shane, and began to lumber toward him.

*Good,* Shane thought. *I'll draw it far away from my mate.*

He snarled, his lips writhing away from his fangs, then began to slowly back away from the grizzly.

The bear growled and charged again. Shane dashed into the woods, taking care not to go too fast. He wanted the bear to keep thinking that he'd catch the panther at any second. He glanced back, satisfied to see that the bear was still in pursuit, and snarled tauntingly. The bear growled and ran faster.

Shane led the bear through the forest, slowing and snarling every time it looked like the bear was losing interest. The sound of the river grew louder as he traveled, but all he could see was trees and bushes.

The bear put on a sudden burst of speed, making Shane work to stay out of reach. He could smell it now, a distinctive scent of fur and musk and fish, and feel its hot breath on his hindquarters. Shane glanced back. The bear was almost on top of him. It lunged, shockingly quick, and swiped at him with a huge paw. Shane took a flying leap forward, crashing through a tall hedge of thorny bushes.

And tumbled through empty air.

He had just enough time to realize that he was falling before he landed. The impact was like hitting concrete, driving the breath from his lungs. Then he was flung forward, tossed about like a toy in rushing, freezing rapids.

Dazed by the impact, unable to breathe, Shane struggled to orient himself.

*You fell off a cliff,* he told himself. *You're in a river. Get your head above the water.*

His muzzle broke the surface. He managed one desperate gulp of air before the current pulled him under.

# CHAPTER TEN

## *Catalina*

Catalina watched from the cave entrance as Shane lured the bear into the woods and out of sight. His panther was so beautiful, fierce and lithe and sleek. Apart from the stab of fear she'd felt when the bear had knocked him down, she wasn't worried about him. He was obviously much faster and more agile than the grizzly, not to mention that he had human intelligence. He'd be back once he'd led the bear far into the woods and then ditched it.

Then a wave of ice-cold terror washed over her, making her hands shake and her guts clench. She suddenly *knew* Shane was in danger. She had to help him.

Catalina scrambled into her clothes and shoes, then grabbed the tranquilizer guns and ran out of the cave. Shane and the bear were nowhere to be seen, but she was certain that she knew which way to go to find him. Catalina bolted toward the woods.

Fear for Shane, the conviction that he was in trouble, and the hope that she could save him drove her as she ran down the hillside and toward the forest. Then, a few feet short of the woods, all those feelings evaporated like a drop of water on a hot pan.

She stumbled to a halt, confused. What had she been thinking? Why had she been so convinced that Shane was in danger? He'd had the situation completely under control the last time she'd seen him. She hadn't heard any yells or had anything else happen to make her think something had gone wrong.

And even if something was wrong, why would she just bolt out without even taking supplies? If Shane was injured, he'd need bandages, maybe a splint, and certainly a fire to keep him warm and ward off shock. She could easily pack everything they had into the medical kit and take it with her.

"Weird," Catalina muttered. Maybe love did strange things to you, like make you suddenly lose your mind when the man you loved turned into a panther and ran off into the woods.

She hesitated at the edge of the forest, wondering if she should go back to the cave to fetch supplies, or back to the cave and stay there. She was tempted to search. But he was almost certainly fine, and if she started wandering around the woods, she'd probably get lost. She might even run straight into the grizzly he'd gotten rid of. It didn't seem like a good idea.

She started to turn to go back, but the skin on the back of her neck prickled an alert. Catalina spun around.

A man stepped out of the woods. It was the shifter who had gotten her scent at the base. The dim light bleached his pale skin to the color of frost, and his hair and eyes were black as midnight.

The tranquilizer guns were in her hands. Catalina fired at him as he rushed her, hitting him once— twice— three times in the chest before he closed with her and wrenched the guns from her hands.

"Shane!" Catalina yelled.

Iron-hard hands yanked her arms behind her back and clamped her wrists. She struggled, then relaxed, realizing that there was no need. She'd hit him three times. He'd collapse any second now.

But he didn't. Instead, he started pushing her forward. She stumbled, off-balance with her arms locked behind her back, and nearly fell.

The man let out an exasperated breath and released one of her arms, but kept a firm grip on her other wrist. Immediately, Catalina tried to stomp on his foot. She moved fast but he moved faster, jerking his foot to the side. She whipped around and tried to punch him in the face.

He caught her wrist before it could connect, holding it in an unbreakable grip. "Fight me again and I'll shoot *you* with the dart gun. It's no trouble for me to carry you back."

She stopped struggling. It was obviously hopeless, and she had no hope of escaping if she was unconscious. "Fine. I surrender."

He released her right wrist but held on to her left. With one hand, he plucked three darts from his chest and dropped them to the ground.

Catalina looked from the darts to his chest. He was wearing a T-shirt, not a bulletproof vest. "Just my luck to get *three* defective darts."

"There's nothing wrong with the darts," he said. "They don't work on me."

"How come?"

"Adrenaline invincibility." At her blank look, he elaborated, "It doesn't matter what you do to me. I won't feel pain, and I won't go down unless you shoot me in the head. With a bullet."

"Oh," Catalina said, enlightened. "I've seen that. A guy who's high on meth or PCP will just keep coming, no matter what you do. It takes five or six people to strap them down in the ER, and then it takes triple doses of sedatives to knock them out."

The man looked annoyed. "I'm not *high*. It's my ultimate predator power. Well, one of them."

Stalling for time but also sincerely curious, Catalina asked, "What's the other one?"

"Tracking. You know that."

"I thought any shifter could track by scent."

"Maybe. But it's not by scent. If it was, you'd have lost me— well, delayed me, anyway— when you went through the creek and climbed those trees. Once I touch you, I can find you anywhere. It's not here." He indicated his nose. "It's here." He tapped his temple.

"That's cool. What does it feel like?"

"It—" He broke off, looking annoyed. "Enough stalling."

He picked up the tranquilizer guns, stuck them in his belt, and started to drag her away.

At the top of her lungs, Catalina yelled, "SHANE! HELP!"

When the echoes of her voice died down, she heard nothing but the sounds of her own feet scuffling through the dead leaves. The man kept on hauling her through the woods.

Catalina felt an unpleasant flutter of fear, for Shane as well as for herself. Noise carried a long way in this sort of country. He couldn't have gotten far away enough to miss her yell in such a short time. In fact, he should have heard her the first time she yelled. And he could run like lightning in his panther form. So where was he?

“Shane!” Catalina shouted again.

“Don’t bother. He’s not coming for you.”

*We’ll see about that,* she thought. *Shane said any shifter can track by scent. And this guy isn’t even bothering to walk through water. Once Shane gets back from wherever he is, he’ll be on us like white on rice.*

As if he had read her mind, the man said, “I don’t mean that he *can’t.* I mean that he *won’t.* Garrity doesn’t come back for people. He’s long gone.”

Indignantly, Catalina burst out, “What do you know about him?”

Her captor turned his cold black gaze on her. “I know enough.”

She fell silent, remembering Shane’s story. He *had* killed for Apex. But not by choice. And he’d eventually decided that he’d rather die than do it again. He’d come back for her.

If he could.

She chewed nervously on her lip, once again worried for him. What had happened to him? Had he been injured in the fight with the bear? He must have been. Or could he have gotten lost? Maybe he could track other people’s scents, but not his own. She hoped that was it.

Despite the dim light and difficult terrain, the man was hurrying her along at a rapid pace. She ought to do something to delay him. It would be much easier for Shane to fight just one enemy, out in the wilderness, than if he didn’t reach her until she was already locked back up in the base.

She considered her options. The man’s grip on her arm was tight as a steel clamp. If she pretended to be sick or hurt, he’d just throw her over his shoulder like a sack of potatoes. They’d probably move even faster if he was carrying her than if they continued walking.

The only thing she could think of was to try to befriend him and persuade him to let her go, which seemed about as likely to succeed as wishing herself a pair of wings to fly away. But she was out of other options, so she said, “My name’s Catalina Mendez. What’s yours?”

“None of your business.”

“None Of Your Business, that’s unusual. Is it a family name?”

He didn’t so much as crack a smile. Nor did he reply. He just kept walking, hauling her along.

*Tactics that don’t work,* she thought. *Number one: small talk. Number two: wisecracks.*

*Let's see if guilt-tripping works better.*

"I'm a paramedic," she said. "I'm not in the military. I didn't sign up for this. I'm a working woman with a family. And friends. And cats. My family is going to think I'm *dead!*"

"Join the club," the man retorted, unmoved.

"Doesn't that bother you?" Catalina asked, now genuinely curious. "Were you kidnapped too?"

That seemed to strike a nerve. He actually stopped, whipping around to face her. "If you ask me one more question, I'll tranquilize you."

She could tell that he meant it. "Okay. Sorry."

He yanked on her arm, dragging her forward again. But she silently exulted. Guilt-tripping was working!

"You know what they're going to do to me, right?" Hastily, she added, "Rhetorical question! I know that you know. They're going to force me to go through the ultimate predator process. It'll probably kill me. Are you okay— oops, question— I mean, please just take a second to think about whether you're really okay with dragging an innocent civilian woman to her *death*."

His voice was no longer cold, but hot with anger as he replied, "Number one, they've improved the process. It's not going to kill you. And number two, don't give me that "oh please save helpless little me" bullshit. You want this."

"I do not!"

He gave a snort of disbelief. "Dr. Elihu showed me some of your test results. Your brain lit up like a Christmas tree whenever he asked you about doing the process or being a hero or any crap like that. You *totally* want to do it."

"If I want it, how come I'm trying to talk you into letting me go?"

He didn't reply immediately, giving Catalina hope. Then he said, "You've got mixed feelings. Just like everybody else. But you're not an innocent victim. And I'm sick of listening to you. Forget questions. If you say one more word of any kind, I'll tranquilize you."

Catalina ground her teeth. She'd been so close!

All the rest of the journey, she tried to think of some plan to delay him or fight him or escape. But nothing came to her, other than hoping that Shane was all right and would catch up to them before they reached the base.

The bright beam of her captor's flashlight picked up the gray concrete of the base. Her heart sank. Shane hadn't come. What had happened to him? He had to be hurt. Badly hurt, or he'd have come anyway. Minor injuries wouldn't have stopped him. Even something like a broken arm wouldn't have stopped him. He was unconscious or couldn't walk or was trapped somewhere. Or he'd been re-captured too. Maybe that was the best option.

Or he was dead.

Catalina flinched away from that thought. She wouldn't believe it. She *didn't* believe it. Either he was also being dragged back to the base, or he'd broken his ankle or something like that and hadn't been able to travel fast enough to catch up with them.

"Home sweet home," her captor said sardonically.

"You won't think it's so funny if I die here."

"I don't know why you keep thinking I care what happens to you," he remarked. "I'm an assassin— a predator— an *animal.* I don't care about anything."

"Then why does it matter that I'm not an innocent victim?"

"Shut up."

He dragged her into the base, where they were greeted by the usual array of guards, and then along the corridors and into the lab.

Dr. Elihu was waiting for them. "Good work. You didn't find Garrity?"

The man shook his head. "He ditched her and took off. I could go back for him, but he's probably long gone."

Dr. Elihu was silent for a moment, looking thoughtfully into the man's black eyes. "No… No. I expect you're right. Don't bother chasing him. I've just got one more job for you, and then you're dismissed. She's ready for ultimate predator now. Bite her."

A jolt of pure adrenaline sang through Catalina's veins. It was finally happening. There was nothing she could do to prevent it. But the thought excited rather than frightened her. In just a few minutes, she'd be a shifter!

She wondered what animal this man could turn into. A bear? A wolf? A panther, like Shane? She hoped for a big cat of some kind. Or else a dragon!

"No." The man folded his arms. "I already told you, I won't do that."

"It's only to protect her. Without shifter healing, she's unlikely to survive the process."

"I don't care."

Dr. Elihu scowled at the man. "Go to your quarters. If she doesn't do well, I'm going to summon you back. We'll see how you feel if she's dying in front of you."

"I. Don't. Care." The man turned around and walked out.

"You're not going to do the process now, right?" Catalina asked uneasily. "There's no point if I won't survive it. You might as well shoot me in the head and be done with it."

The doctor gave her an icy stare. "Oh, no, we're doing it. He'll come around. And even if he doesn't, your experience will provide valuable data that will be useful for our next try."

*"Valuable data" like my death.*

Hot fury flashed through her. Catalina punched Dr. Elihu square in the nose, throwing her full weight behind the blow. The force of the strike jarred her entire body, and the doctor fell on his ass.

"How dare you!" Dr. Elihu shouted from the floor. His voice was thick and choked, and blood ran down his chin.

Catalina laughed. Then a sharp pain stung her shoulder. One of the guards had nailed her with a dart. She slid to the ground, paralyzed. People walked in and out of her field of vision, and then she was unceremoniously hefted on to a cold metal table.

*This is really it,* she thought. *I should be terrified.*

But she wasn't. Part of her simply couldn't believe that she was actually going to die. Shane would rescue her, or that strange shifter would change his mind and bite her after all, or she'd simply be lucky and beat the odds. But another part, which did accept the possibility that this could be the end, was filled not with fear, but with sadness for everyone who would mourn for her.

*My family,* she thought. *My kitties. Ellie. And Shane— what will it do to him if* another *person he loves dies here?*

Then darkness swept her away, and all her thoughts with it.

# CHAPTER ELEVEN

## *Shane*

Shane fought his way up through the rapids, snatching gulps of air when he could, trying to keep himself afloat. The current slammed him into a boulder, knocking the breath from his lungs. But he didn't panic. He'd been trained for exactly this sort of situation. Instead, he let the river carry him downstream, not trying to fight for air, until his diaphragm relaxed and he could breathe again.

He swam at an angle so he wasn't directly battling the current, trying to make his way to the bank. Once he came almost close enough to touch it, only to be flung back into the middle of the rapids. But Shane persisted, though even his strong panther's muscles burned with exertion, until his outstretched paw touched sand. He clambered ashore, then collapsed on the bank, exhausted and sodden and chilled.

He lay coughing and gasping for a minute, then shook the water from his fur and looked around. He was at the base of a cliff so steep he doubted even his panther could climb it, and on the wrong side of the river to even try. Shane didn't want to swim those rapids again if he could help it. And he'd been carried far downstream. He could be as much as a mile away.

*At least the bear has to be gone,* he thought. *But what's Catalina going to do when I don't come back?*

He hoped she'd stay put and wait for him. Without enhanced shifter senses or special training, she'd have no way of tracking him and would only get lost herself.

He stood up, shook himself again, and set out along the bank, walking upstream. The sooner he got back, the less likely she was to get worried enough to decide that looking for him was the best of bad alternatives.

Shane set a brisk pace, loping along the bank as the sky brightened from indigo to blue. He finally spotted a tall hedge at the top of the cliff that he thought marked the place where he'd fallen. But the river raged beside him, and he didn't want to risk getting swept downstream again if he tried to swim it.

Frustrated, Shane kept heading upstream, hoping the current would get less fierce. It didn't, but he came to a place where several boulders protruded above the waterline. They were wet and looked slippery, but they seemed like his best chance. Shane leaped from one boulder to the next, landing lightly and launching again before he had a chance to slip, until he made it to the other side of the river.

And the cliff.

It loomed before him, very high and nearly vertical. His panther could climb any tree in existence, digging his claws deep into the bark, but this cliff was something else entirely.

*Well?* Shane asked his panther.

He felt the big cat's reluctance to admit to weakness, a trait matched by his own. But after lifting a paw to test the rock surface, his panther admitted, *I'd fall right back in the river.*

Shane considered hiking further in the hope that the cliff would get more climbable. But he'd already been gone for an hour, at least. Catalina would be worried. If he was gone for long enough, she'd start searching for him— in an area that already contained one pissed-off grizzly bear.

Shane became a man again. Nude and shivering in the cold dawn wind, he looked up at the forbidding cliff.

"Here goes," he said, and began to climb.

He'd gone rock-climbing before. It was a hobby of Destiny's, and she'd often invited the entire team to accompany her for a climb and a picnic. And of course he'd climbed on obstacle courses and rappelled down. But even the rugged outdoors climbing Destiny enjoyed had been nothing like this. For one thing, he'd had ropes to prevent him from falling to his death if he slipped. For another thing, he'd been wearing clothes. He had to press himself right into the rough cliff-face to keep his balance, which was painful in at least three different ways for his most sensitive areas.

*Protect your mate,* his panther reminded him.

Shane clung to the cliff, his fingers and toes jammed into narrow cracks, and muttered aloud, "Just because it hurts doesn't mean I'm giving up."

He clambered upward, not looking down. Often he was forced to balance on only one foot, with one hand clinging to a smooth knob of stone.

A piece of granite broke off under his foot. He dropped down with a terrifying jolt, catching himself with three fingers on his right hand. For a precarious moment, he hung on, supporting his own body weight with those fingers alone. Sweating, he felt around for a new foothold. His searching toes found a crack. Shane crammed them into it, caught his breath, and then reached up for the next handhold.

Shane could hardly believe it when he finally hauled himself over the edge of the cliff. He became a panther so he could again leap over the bushes— no way was he shoving through those thorns naked— and began retracing his path back toward the cave.

But when he reached the cave, he found it empty. Catalina had gone, taking the tranquilizer guns and one set of her own clothes but leaving everything else. He nosed at his discarded jeans, and gave a huff of dismay when he found his Swiss Army knife and lighter still in the pocket. If she'd set out to rescue him, wouldn't she have taken those?

Wouldn't she have taken everything? She was a paramedic— she'd have been prepared to find him injured. She could have used the extra clothing for bandages, the lighter to make a fire to keep him warm, and the knife for anything to make a splint to perform emergency field surgery. His mate wouldn't have just rushed out unprepared. She was brave, but not reckless.

He sniffed, picking up her freshest scent trail, and followed it out of the cave. At the edge of the woods, it was joined by that of another human. Fury made his hackles raise as he realized that she'd been captured. He didn't recognize the other person's scent, but that wasn't a surprise; it must be someone who'd started working for Apex since Shane had escaped a year ago or whom he'd never scented as a panther.

Some shifters could scent people while they were in human form, but Shane couldn't.

He let out a hiss of anger and concern when he caught sight of three emptied tranquilizer darts on the ground. Had someone actually shot her three times? Or had she managed to hit her attacker?

But both the scent trails led back into the woods; Catalina and her kidnapper were both on their feet. Shane puzzled over the darts, then gave up on that small mystery. The important thing was to catch up with them before they made it back to the base.

Shane followed the trail through the woods, moving as fast as he could. But in his heart, he was certain that he was too late. The sun shone bright through the leaves; he was hours behind them.

As he loped through the woods, he considered the best strategy. Infiltrate the base? Wait till someone left the base, ambush them and get their phone, call Protection, Inc., and *then* infiltrate the base? Shane liked that idea. He needed reinforcements, for sure, but he didn't have to wait to rescue his mate till they arrived.

He sensed approval from his panther, both of the ambush and the infiltration.

*Hiding in shadows,* hissed the big cat, with the implication that it was always a good choice.

Then a jolt of cold terror made his heart lurch and his fur stand on end.

*Protect Catalina,* his panther hissed urgently.

Shane put on a burst of speed, even though he didn't know what had gotten into him and his panther. He'd always known Catalina was in danger; there was no reason to think it was imminent right now.

*Mates know,* his panther told him. *She's in danger* now. *Don't infiltrate. Don't ambush. Just run!*

Shane ran through the forest. He'd never heard before that mates knew if the other was in trouble, but he believed it. He could feel its truth in his bones.

The gray concrete of the base came into sight, so much less threatening from the outside than it was on the inside. Shane forced himself to halt, making a quick survey from the shadows of the trees. Given time, he could sneak in, ambush some guards, obtain clothes and weapons…

… but time was the one thing he didn't have.

Shane became a man and walked out of the woods with his hands raised. He made himself go slowly, giving the guards monitoring the video feeds plenty of time to see him and alert their superiors. The last thing he needed was to be tranquilized.

Once he was within earshot, he called, "I surrender! Tell Dr. Elihu I'll do whatever he wants, so long as he doesn't hurt Catalina."

By the time he reached the door, his message had been received and answered. The door slid open, revealing ten armed guards.

One, looking embarrassed, tossed him a jacket. "Tie this around your waist."

If Shane hadn't been so worried, he'd have been amused. He tied it on, concealing his nudity, and said, "I want to see Catalina."

The guards didn't reply. Instead, they began hurrying him along the corridors. Shane went with them, his nightmare replaying in his mind. Justin, gasping for breath in his arms. Catalina, dying...

The door slid open. Shane forced himself not to lunge inside and give some trigger-happy guard an excuse to knock him out. Instead, he took a single step forward.

The scene that met his eyes so exactly resembled his nightmare that Shane froze in the doorway. Catalina lay ashen and gasping on a hospital bed, surrounded by doctors, nurses, and machines. She was hooked up to so many tubes and wires that she seemed caught in some horrific spider's web.

He'd come too late.

Shane bolted forward, forgetting the guards. His heart was pounding so loudly in his ears that he couldn't hear the hum of the machines or the urgent voices of the doctors, but only saw lights flashing and lips moving.

Catalina's eyes were open. Frightened. His mate was one of the bravest people he'd ever met, and she was lying there afraid and dying.

Shane sank down on his knees beside the bed and took her hand. It was limp and cold. Lifeless. The wires that attached to it were warmer than her skin.

"Hold on," he urged her. "You're strong. You can get through this. Fight!"

But he could see in her pallor and hear in her breathing that no amount of courage and determination would save her. Justin had been brave and Elizabeth had been determined and all of them had fought like hell, and it hadn't saved any of them.

He couldn't save her, but he wouldn't leave her.

Shane laid his head beside hers and whispered, "I love you. I'll stay with you to the end. You won't die alone."

She had no breath to reply, but some of the fear went out of her eyes. The extraordinary woman he loved was dying, and all he could do for her was give her that small comfort. He squeezed her hand and stroked her hair, his heart cold as a lump of stone within his chest. Shane had known her for such a short time, but he couldn't imagine what it would be like to live without her.

The part of him that was pure predator thought, *Maybe I won't have to. Once she dies, I'll kill as many of them as I can before they take me down.*

A hand descended on his shoulder. Shane knocked it away with a hiss.

Distantly, he heard a man yelp in pain. Then Dr. Elihu stepped into his field of vision, flapping his arms to get Shane's attention. From the rasp of his voice, he'd been shouting at Shane for some time without Shane hearing him.

"Bite her!" Dr. Elihu demanded. "What are you waiting for? It's the only thing that might save her life!"

Shane stared at the doctor, jarred out of despair. "I thought she'd been bitten already, *before* you did the process. Your other shifter—"

"Wouldn't do it," the doctor replied. "Bite her, or she dies."

A wild hope sprang up in Shane. He turned back to Catalina. "Should I? It could kill you—"

She gave him a look that didn't need words: *Yes, you idiot.*

The next instant, he was a panther. He was sitting on the floor with his huge black paws resting on the bed, one of them pinning down Catalina's wrist. Shane bent down and bit her hand.

When he became a man again, he could still taste the copper of her blood. He wiped his mouth with the back of his hand, then slid one arm beneath her shoulders, gazing into her glassy eyes. Waiting.

It happened fast if it was going to happen. Either way, it happened fast. One second Elizabeth had been standing with blood soaking into her boot, and the next she was a leopard, holding up one crimson-stained paw and lashing her spotted tail.

One second Mason had been wincing and applying pressure to a bite wound on his forearm, and the next he was dead on the floor.

"Shane…!" Catalina's voice was hoarse but strong.

*It's working,* he thought, his heart pounding. *I hope…*

A sudden weight pressed down on his arm and shoved at his chest. Thin cloth over smooth skin became soft fur over lithe muscle.

A magnificent leopard sprawled over the bed, its emerald eyes bright and alert. She nuzzled his hand, and he rubbed behind her ears. As Shane kept stroking her, a rumble filled the room. She was purring.

Fur smoothed into skin, and Catalina lay nude on the bed. She hastily grabbed the sheet and yanked it back up.

She had the strength to pull the sheet over herself. Her color was better. She was breathing easily.

Catalina wasn't going to die. She'd already gone through the ultimate predator process, and she wasn't dying.

His mate would live.

His mate would *live.*

"I was a leopard," Catalina said, her eyes filled with wonder. Excitedly, she added, "And I'll have super-powers now, right?"

Shane had to smile at how thrilled she sounded, when thirty seconds ago she'd been dying. That was his fearless mate. "The powers come later. It might take a couple days."

Catalina reached up to stroke his hair. "I knew you'd come back for me."

Shane held her in his arms, resting his head against hers. He closed his eyes, reveling in the ease of her breathing, the steady thump of her heart, the warmth of her skin. He'd thought she was lost to him, but here she was. He didn't care that they were once again imprisoned or that he'd missed the chance to alert his team. Nothing mattered but that Catalina was alive.

An annoying voice penetrated his awareness, speaking louder and louder. Shane paid no attention to it, not even enough to listen to what it was saying. But it finally reached such a pitch that, without opening his eyes, he snapped, "What?"

Catalina cleared her throat. "I think Dr. Elihu is trying to tell you to put on some pants."

# CHAPTER TWELVE

## *Catalina*

To Catalina's annoyance, Shane was escorted out once a medical technician fetched him some clothes. At least she got to watch him get dressed. She hadn't been able to appreciate it properly when he'd rushed in mostly naked, given that she'd been dying at the time.

Catalina spent the day recovering and getting medical tests done in the lab, and then Dr. Elihu grudgingly agreed to release her back to her room. Before he let her leave, he told her all about the agonizing way she'd die if she ran away now. As the doctor described the precise symptoms, Catalina's heart lurched at the realization of just how much Shane had understated when he'd told her his story.

Dr. Elihu, who had been closely watching her face, looked satisfied. He'd obviously mistaken her expression of horror at what Shane had suffered for one of terror at what might befall herself.

*Oh, well,* Catalina thought. *It's for the best. Now he thinks I won't try to escape. Maybe he'll let down his guard.*

"How often do I need the treatment?" she asked.

"We'll do it once a week to be safe," Dr. Elihu replied. "But it varies from person to person. The range seems to be seven to twelve days. But you don't want to find out the hard way what your maximum is."

Catalina eyed him thoughtfully. It had been terrible and dangerous, but Shane had survived with no treatments at all.

Apparently her thought appeared on another neon sign, because the doctor said, "Garrity would have died the first time he ran away if we hadn't found him in time. I believe that his body slowly adjusted to the process over time, enabling him to live without the treatments by the time he ran again. Even so, he almost died, didn't he?"

Before she could stop herself, Catalina nodded.

"I thought so." The doctor practically glowed with smugness. His nose was still swollen and red. Catalina wanted to punch him again. "So if you run away now, you certainly won't survive. If you waited a year, you might have a chance. But I doubt it. I suspect that Garrity was a special case."

Catalina tried very hard to keep *"We'll see about that"* from lighting up over her head.

"And he knows it," Dr. Elihu went on, staring hard at her. "Ask him how long he thinks you'd last away from Apex. If he cares about you at all, he won't help you run away again."

He snapped his fingers at the guards, and they escorted her back to her room. Catalina kept her gaze fixed on the floor so her face wouldn't betray her. She had no intention of staying on the base one second longer than she had to— not when she could turn into a leopard!

She suppressed a grin at the memory of her body expanding, her senses sharpening, and the luxurious sense of stretching as she'd first extended her claws.

*I'm a ferocious big cat*, she thought. *Wonder what my kitties will think?*

The guards opened the door barely wide enough for her to squeeze in, shoved her through, and slammed it behind her.

Catalina stumbled. She started to fling out her arms to catch herself. But as her weight shifted forward, she suddenly knew that she had alternatives beyond regaining her balance or falling down. Out of the corner of her eye, she saw Shane jumping up to grab for her shoulder. He was as fast as always. If she'd continued to fall, he'd have caught her with time to spare.

But she was already moving, even faster than him, sliding beneath his outstretched hand in a controlled dive. She twisted in mid-air and landed lightly in a crouch at the other end of the room.

It was a leap worthy of an Olympic gymnast. And it had been easy. Instinctive, even. She was already standing upright before Shane even had time to turn around.

Catalina flexed her hands, then rotated her shoulders, ankles, and hips. Her entire body felt different: stronger, lighter, more flexible, more aware of her position in space. Her senses were different as well, subtly sharper and more perceptive. Light was brighter. Colors were more distinct. Sounds were more clear.

Shane stood across the room from her, a boyish grin she'd never seen before brightening his face. She could feel the radiant heat coming off his body. As usual, he had his shirt off, but now she could perceive the difference in temperature between his exposed torso and his jeans-clad lower body. She could scent him, too, an intoxicating aroma of clean sweat and masculine musk and a faint trace of something green and herbal, like fresh-cut grass.

Her leopard spoke within her, in a strong yet distinctly feminine purr. *My mate.*

Catalina had loved and desired Shane before. But before she'd become a shifter herself, she'd had doubts. He loved her, that she knew. But she hadn't been sure if it would work out between them. She'd seen lots of love affairs flare up between people working together in disaster zones, and she'd seen most of them burn out once they both returned to their normal lives. Catalina had hoped that what she and Shane had together was based on more than their circumstances and would last after they returned home, but she hadn't had any way to know for sure.

Now she knew that he would never leave her. With all her heart and soul, with the pure instinct of the leopard that now lived inside her, Catalina knew that Shane wasn't just her lover, but her mate. They were meant to be together. Theirs was a bond that would live as long as they did.

Desire broke over her like a tidal wave. She was instantly wet, hot and slippery between the thighs, her clit throbbing like a heartbeat. Catalina squirmed, and just the little friction from her thighs rubbing together was enough to make her gasp. Her pulse hummed in her ears, too fast to feel individual beats. She couldn't catch her breath. Her whole body burned for Shane. She was dying of thirst, and he was a tall, cool glass of water. If she didn't have him this instant, she'd die of longing.

She knew, she *knew* that Shane felt the same way— she could see it in the heat of his eyes, in the set of his jaw, in every line of his body— but he took a step away from her, not toward her. Catalina couldn't believe it. As she watched, incredulous, he took another step backward. Then another, until he stood with his back to the wall, relaxed and casual as if he had nothing better to do than simply *lean*.

A growl of impatience rumbled through her chest and throat. "What are you doing? Are you *playing* with me?"

He nodded, a teasing smile hovering at his lips.

*Like a cat plays with a mouse,* she thought. *No, like a cat plays with another cat.*

His voice was low and rough, half-growl, half purr. "If you want me, come and get me."

Catalina leaped. But Shane was ready for her this time. He stepped forward to meet her, and his deft hands snatched her out of the air. For a breathless moment, he swung her around as if she was light as a feather. Then they were tumbling down, rolling over and over on the floor, tearing at each other's clothes. His hands were urgent, his scent dizzying, his breath coming in shuddering gasps. She could feel every place where his body touched hers, hot and vivid as a fever dream.

Catalina heard herself groan as she tore the shirt from his body. She was out of control, ripping his clothes to shreds and digging her nails into his back. No longer cool, Shane made a sound that was almost a snarl as he ripped her shirt off. It tore straight down the middle, along with her bra. He buried his face in her breasts, licking and nipping and kissing. His tongue left trails of fire on her skin.

She thrust against him, rubbing herself over his rock-hard shaft. He lifted his head and reached down, yanking her jeans off. Her panties tore in his hands, leaving him with shreds of thin, damp cloth that smelled like her. She was throbbing, desperate, dripping wet. Her hands shook as they fumbled at his jeans. She couldn't get the button undone.

"Allow me," Shane purred.

He slipped his hand between her thighs. She bucked against his fingers, barely noticing that he was sliding his jeans off with one hand while his other moved between her slick folds. All her senses were heightened almost to the point of pain, smell and touch, sight and sound and touch. His briefest caress was brought her to the point of climax, trembling and crying out. Her inner walls pulsed against his fingers as her orgasm rocketed up her spine.

Dazed, Catalina blinked hard, clearing her vision. Her climax had taken the edge off her urgency, but she wasn't satisfied. She still *wanted.*

"I don't know what's happened to me," she muttered. "I've never felt like this before. Not even with you."

"You're a shifter now," Shane said. She could feel his stuttering breath against her face as he spoke; he wasn't quite as cool as he sounded. "A new shifter. New senses. It takes some getting used to."

Her hands clenched around his muscular shoulders. "I don't want to get used to it."

"Good." Shane was naked now, poised above her, his cock a steel rod against her thighs. "Ready for more?"

She might have said yes, or might have simply pulled him toward her. His scent and heat were all around her, making it hard to think. He drove into her, filling her with his hard shaft. She arched into him, wet and more than ready. Every exhaled breath as he pushed into her rumbled through his chest, vibrating against hers in low snarls that became shorter, fiercer, more urgent with every thrust. She didn't know what sounds she was making, but she saw in the blaze in Shane's ice-blue eyes that he heard them, and they set him on fire.

He bit down on her shoulder, harder than he had the last time. Now she instinctively knew what that meant. He was marking her as his mate, driven irresistibly by the instinct of the panther within him. Catalina turned her head and nipped him back, marking him in turn.

"Mine," he growled.

*Mine,* came an echoing purr within her.

The next thrust sent the bright flash of orgasm through her nerves. Catalina came again and again like a string of firecrackers was going off inside her body, each orgasm bursting on the heels of the next. It was almost too much to bear, but she didn't want it to end. The last climax exploded up from her clit and rolled through her body, leaving her limp and trembling in Shane's arms.

He stroked the wet hair from her forehead. "How was that?"

"How do you think?" Her voice, which she had meant to be light and teasing, came out shaky.

He tilted his head and frowned as if giving it genuine consideration, then allowed, "Probably not disappointing."

Catalina laughed. "Is it always going to be like this? Or am I going to get used to my shifter senses?"

He kissed her. "Sex with you is always going to be amazing. As for the shifter senses, if the thrill does wear off after a while, I'll just have to try harder to keep it exciting for you."

Her mind reeled at the idea of Shane making an extra effort to keep it exciting. "I'll hold you to that."

They lay together for a while, but as the afterglow wore off, Catalina became filled with a restless energy. She couldn't relax, but kept squirming and fidgeting. She had to try out her new powers.

She got up and dressed, then began moving about the room, tumbling and leaping, light as a feather and agile as a cat. It was as if she was in zero gravity. Her sense of her own body and its capacity to move in space was true and unerring as a compass needle pointing north. She could tumble through the air as easily as she could walk.

Shane lay still and watched her, his gaze appreciative. She didn't know which she enjoyed more, her own new agility or the admiration and enjoyment that lit up his cool blue eyes. It made her want to show off for him.

Catalina jumped high rather than across, reaching up to slap her hand against the ceiling. Her hand struck harder than she had intended, opening a small crack. Plaster dust drifted down, sprinkling her upturned face as she landed.

*Not just super-agility,* she thought. *Super-strength.*

She saw in Shane's expression that he had the same thought that she did. But his voice was casual as he asked, "Like your power?"

"I like it a *lot*," she replied.

She started toward the main door, intending to try her strength on the bolt, but Shane shook his head.

"Let's try something more discreet." He beckoned her into the bathroom, where he indicated the steel towel rack. "Try this."

Catalina laid her hands on it. As she applied steady pressure, she caught sight of herself in the mirror. She looked the same as she ever had: black hair, brown eyes, brown skin, big breasts, plump arms. But the solid steel rod bent under her hands.

Her palms were sweating with effort. They slipped. Catalina instinctively grabbed harder, and the towel rack tore out of the wall.

Shane was standing right behind her, bracing her before she could fall.

He caught her gaze in the mirror, his expression intent and thoughtful. She knew that look: his wheels were turning.

"Dr. Elihu really screwed up when he gave me powers," she said, grinning. Having a super-power was every bit as exciting as she'd ever dreamed it would be. "This room can't hold us any longer. If we combine our strength, you and me together could rip the door right out of the wall."

Shane didn't smile back. "We could. But escaping isn't so simple now."

"Because of the treatment I need?" Catalina recounted her conversation with Dr. Elihu, concluding, "But he'd say anything to make me stay. What I know for sure is that you can survive without the treatment. If you can, there's a good chance I can too."

Shane was silent, but his eyes were the blue of a frozen lake, as bleak as they'd been when he'd knelt by her bed and stopped telling her to fight, the moment when he'd whispered that he loved her. Only then had she been truly convinced that all hope was lost and she was going to die.

But she hadn't.

She cupped his face in her hands. "Hey. It'll be all right. You saved me, remember? You can save me again. Take me to Dr. Bedford— she kept you alive. It won't be fun, but I'll make it. I'm tough."

"I know you are." Shane's muscles moved under her palms as he swallowed. "If you're sure you want to risk it, I'll break you out of here."

"Do it. I don't want them to make me do what they made you do," Catalina said. She thought, but didn't add, *And I don't want you to stay here to protect me.*

"You're right." He nodded, resolve hardening his features. "They won't do that to you. They won't do it to anyone again, if I— if *we*— can help it."

"So how do we stop them?"

Catalina wasn't surprised when he spoke immediately and with confidence. Of course he had a plan. Shane always had a plan.

"I don't think Dr. Elihu shares his research," Shane said. "He seems like the type who'd keep it to himself. If we destroy his lab and all the files in it, we should be able to shut down ultimate predator for good. So all we need to do is break out of this room in the middle of the night— if you're taken to the lab tomorrow, Dr. Elihu will notice that you've gotten your powers— get to his lab without getting tranquilized, trash it before anyone can stop us, and run like hell."

"All we need to do," Catalina echoed teasingly. "You sure there isn't anything else?"

She could see that Shane got the joke, but he didn't smile. "There is. I'll try to download the data and take it with us before we destroy everything, in case we can recreate the treatment outside of Apex. But I'm not sure if that'll be possible. It's not just that the equipment might only exist in Apex. I'm not a hacker, and it could take hours to break into the system."

"As opposed to minutes to just break the system?"

He nodded. "I won't know till we get there. But I'll try."

"Don't try too long. I'd rather risk dying outside than being trapped here forever."

"So would I."

He took her in his arms. They made love again, tender and fierce, losing themselves in sensation and touch and ecstasy, whiling away the hours of the night.

***

They didn't sleep, but lay in each other's arms, waiting until Catalina's watch said 3:00 AM.

"My favorite time of day," she whispered to Shane. "Night. Day."

"Mine too," he whispered back. "It's the best time to hunt."

They both took hold of the door lock, a massive steel contraption. Shane's hands looked huge beside hers.

"Three," said Shane. "Two. One. *Pull.*"

She threw herself back with all her strength. Shane gave a grunt of effort, his muscles bulging.

The door tore out of the wall.

Six guards stood outside. Shane pounced on them before Catalina had done more than stagger backward. He punched one in the jaw and snatched the tranquilizer gun from his belt, then fired at another guard without missing a beat. His gun hand was swinging to level on the third by the time Catalina got it together to move.

She leaped at the nearest guard, and felt a surge of triumph when she hit him. But even while using her agility, she'd forgotten her new strength. She slammed into the guard with a startlingly hard impact. Both of them flew forward and hit the wall.

Catalina staggered to her feet, bruised and shaken. Four guards were down, including one beneath her. Of the remaining two, one was opening his mouth to shout, and the other was firing at Shane. Her instinct was to go for the one trying to hurt her mate, but she recalled Shane's advice on not jumping in front of him when he was trying to shoot someone.

Her moment of decision felt long to her, but it passed in a fraction of a second. She leaped toward the guard trying to shout. Catalina hurtled easily through the air, tucking herself into a ball for more speed and then uncurling just before she reached her target. This time she'd judged her powers better. Her hand clapped over the guard's mouth as she landed beside him. He struggled, but his yell was muffled by her hand.

Shane dropped to the floor. The dart fired by the remaining guard passed over his head and smacked into the wall. Shane rolled forward, reached out with his free hand, grabbed the guard by the ankle, and yanked. The guard fell with a thud. Still lying on the floor, Shane fired first at the guard fighting Catalina, then at the one he'd pulled down.

A moment later, all the guards lay unconscious.

"Good call," remarked Shane. Catalina was gasping from exertion and excitement, but he was as cool as ever. "And good work. How was your first fight?"

It had been primal and thrilling. Her inner predator had taken over, making every movement instinctive. Though she'd felt the danger, she'd felt confident in her abilities, too. Fighting had felt natural, as if it had been what she'd been born to do. But most of all, fighting beside her mate had satisfied some deep need within her. It was as if a piece of her life that she'd never even realized she'd been missing had unexpectedly clicked into place, making her whole at last.

Deep inside her, Catalina's leopard purred her approval. *We* are *predators. Mates hunt together.*

"Wow," Catalina managed.

Shane bent and gave her the quickest of kisses, a bare brush of his lips against hers. It made her head spin even more.

"That's my mate," he said. "Let's go fight some more."

He led her down the corridors. More guards were waiting. The next two fights passed in a confused rush of adrenaline. Catalina knocked out one guard, and then another. None managed to sound the alarm. Shane never let anyone so much as touch her, though he took some hard blows protecting her.

The next thing she knew, they stood in another empty corridor. She had lost track of where they were, but Shane hadn't.

"Next turn goes to the corridor the lab's on," he whispered into her ear. "I'll go first. They won't see me until it's too late. Give me a count of ten, then come in."

Catalina nodded. Shane's eyes narrowed in concentration. She didn't see any change in him, but he walked around the corner as casually as if he was strolling to the grocery store.

She gritted her teeth as she counted to ten. She wasn't afraid that he was in danger; she knew he could handle it. But she was sorry to miss seeing him in action.

At the last count, she stepped around the corner. Three guards lay unconscious on the floor, while a fourth was starting to flee. Catalina leaped forward, firing the tranquilizer gun in mid-air. The dart smacked into the last guard's back. He took one more step, then fell unconscious.

"Show-off," Shane said softly.

"You love it," Catalina whispered back.

He plucked off a fallen guard's badge and waved it at the lock. The door slid open.

Catalina tensed to leap, but Shane was faster. His tranquilizer pistol instantly leveled on the man who stepped into the lab, the black-haired, dark-eyed shifter who had tracked and captured her.

She waited for the men to attack each other. Instead, they took one look at each other, then froze. The only motion in the room was that of the door as it slid shut behind her kidnapper, leaving the three of them alone together.

# CHAPTER THIRTEEN

## *Shane*

Shane felt as if he'd turned a corner and walked straight out of reality. Everything around him fell out of his awareness: the lab, the danger, the mission. He could barely feel the warmth of his mate, though she was standing right beside him.

*It can't be,* Shane thought.

But there was that face he knew as well as his own. Justin's face, with its sharp cheekbones, strong chin, and mouth that used to always be grinning or quivering with poorly-suppressed amusement, waiting for a prank to be sprung. The same body, tall and strong, though he held himself differently now. Justin used to be relaxed and unhurried, even in combat. Now he had an edgy predator's wariness that made the air around him vibrate with danger.

The hair was wrong. It should be copper as a new penny, and instead it was black. The *eyes* were wrong. They should be a startlingly bright green, and instead they were dark as mirrors in an empty room. Justin's skin should be tanned, but it was pale as if it had been a long time since he'd spent time in the sun.

But Shane could never mistake his friend, even if he'd changed much more than that.

He opened his mouth to say, *"But you're dead."*

Before he could speak, the penny dropped and he tried to change it to, *"They told me you were dead."*

Both sentences caught in his throat and choked him.

"You never came back for me." It was Justin's voice, but with a chill that Shane had never heard before, in all the ten years they'd served together in combat. "'Never leave a fallen comrade.' I knew you'd come for me. But you didn't. I finally had to admit to myself that you weren't going to."

Catalina's baffled tones rose up clear into the silence. "Who are you? I thought you were one of Apex's guys. Shane's buddies all died… I thought," she added doubtfully.

Shane finally managed to speak. He meant to explain everything— he knew what had to have happened— but all that came out was the name that had been stuck on the tip of his tongue ever since the door had opened. "Red?"

"*Justin?*" Catalina exclaimed.

Justin nodded, but Shane couldn't read those dark eyes. He'd always known what Justin was thinking. It was like talking to a stranger with the face of a friend.

"Your hair," Shane said, only realizing the absurdity of the words as they left his lips.

But Justin responded as if it was the most natural question in the world. "I dye it. My natural color is too eye-catching. It makes people notice me. Remember me. The sort of missions Apex sends me on, I should blend into a crowd."

"And your eyes," Shane began, then caught himself. "Of course. Contacts."

Justin shook his head. "They're real. It was a side effect of ultimate predator."

"I thought you were dead." Now that Shane could speak again, the words burst out like a flash flood. "I saw you die! I *felt* it. You stopped breathing. You didn't have a pulse. I was giving you CPR, but the doctors wanted to take over. They tried to pull me off you. I wouldn't let go. A guard hit me across the face, and I still wouldn't. They had to tranquilize me. When I woke up, they told me you were dead. I…"

Shane shook his head, feeling foolish. "It never occurred to me to doubt it. Everyone else had died. I assumed the process killed everyone."

Some flicker of expression crossed Justin's half-familiar face, but Shane couldn't tell what it was.

"You know Shane," Catalina put in. "Justin, think about it. You *know* him. You've known him for much longer than I have. Is he the sort of person who would ever leave anybody behind?"

"No," Justin said, as if automatically. "No. But you didn't come back. And I knew you had the choice to stay away. Blackburn bit you, but you escaped before they could put you through the ultimate predator process. At least… That's what they told me."

Shane was starting to be able to read his expressions. Some echo of the man he used to know stirred, breaking through the chill. A spark of anger rose in those strange eyes.

"Those assholes!" Justin exclaimed. *That* was more like him. "They lied to both of us. They told you I died so you wouldn't look for me. And they told me you'd abandoned me so *I* wouldn't look for *you*."

Shane nodded. A cold fury was rising in him as well, pushing aside the shock. "They must have kept us in different bases so we wouldn't run into each other accidentally. Then they re-captured me, and my mate here got caught with me. They were probably going to move us to a different base, to keep me away from you, but she and I escaped first. They must have been pretty desperate to send you after me."

Justin didn't smile, but his forehead creased with faint amusement. "They were. Their best search teams got nowhere. They told me you'd broken into the base, grabbed their new recruit, and taken off."

"Never," swore Shane. "I wouldn't leave a wounded comrade. I wouldn't leave a wounded stranger. I wouldn't leave Catalina. I wouldn't have left you. And I won't leave you now."

"I know." Justin sounded like he was being choked. "I think I always knew, deep down. My *leopard* believed in you! But I wouldn't listen."

"Join us. I'm going to try to download the data for ultimate predator, so Catalina can live away from here. Then we'll destroy it, so it can never be used again." Shane indicated a bank of computers.

"Oh, you don't need the data," Justin said. "Catalina went through 2.0. Dr. Elihu lied about why it's different. It's just as likely to kill you as 1.0. The improvement is that if you survive, it adapts to you. She doesn't need any treatments. He was going to do fake ones so she'd think she needs to stay here to survive."

The relief Shane felt at this nearly made him dizzy. He looked to Catalina for her reaction, but she looked no more than ordinarily pleased. His brave mate had already known she'd have the strength and will to survive, no matter what.

The three of them didn't need to discuss what they'd do next. They trashed the lab as fast as they could, smashing computers and rummaging for data drives to destroy. Now that he wasn't so worried about Catalina, Shane could relax and enjoy the sight of his amazing mate tearing metal with her bare hands.

Justin started opening bottles and pouring liquid over all the electronic equipment. Shane caught the scent of an inflammable cleaner.

"Got a match?" Shane asked.

Justin shook his head.

"I'll look for a lighter," Catalina volunteered.

"No need," Shane said. "I can start it with a spark. Hold on."

He surveyed the room. Everything seemed destroyed, but Justin was right to make sure Apex couldn't salvage any data. Shane started to lead Catalina toward Justin, so they'd be on the same side of the lab when they set the fire.

Shouts and approaching footsteps sounded from several directions at once. Justin was perfectly positioned to torch the lab and get away before more enemies arrived. So was Shane, with Catalina. But once either of them set the lab on fire, the flames would separate them.

Shane and Justin looked at each other. It was if no time at all had passed between missions, and they were once again in combat together.

"Meet you outside," said Shane.

There was no time for anything else. Justin snapped two wires and crouched, ready to touch them together.

"Go!" he shouted.

Shane grabbed Catalina's arm and hauled her out the door. A puff of hot air rippled against his back as the lab went up in flames.

A startled guard jumped back from the corridor they entered. He was the only person who met them. Shane tranquilized him, and then he and Catalina ran down the corridor. It was lined with closed doors and blind turns, perfect for an ambush. Shane kept glancing backward as he ran, slowing him down. With her new agility and strength, Catalina instinctively ran faster, getting ahead of him. Too far ahead.

As he started to speed up to catch up with her, a flicker of movement caught Shane's eye. He spun around. As he did so, Dr. Elihu stepped out silently from around a corner. He had a bulletproof vest strapped over his doctor's coat, and he was aiming a pistol at Catalina.

Shane was too far from Catalina to throw himself over her. He was closer to the doctor, but still too far to jump him.

As a man.

Shane became a panther and leaped at Dr. Elihu. A hard impact slammed into his chest in mid-air, and then he knocked the doctor down. Dr. Elihu's gun went flying. Shane crouched atop him, snarling. At last, he was face-to-face with his enemy.

The doctor flinched, then regained control of himself. His lips curled in a familiar contemptuous sneer. "You wouldn't dare kill me. I'm the only person in the world who knows how to keep your girlfriend alive."

*Liar,* his panther hissed. *Kill him.*

Shane snarled again. It would be so satisfying to sink his fangs into Dr. Elihu's throat…

…but it would be quick, too. He wouldn't suffer. After the ruin he'd brought to others, the lives he'd taken and broken, Shane wanted to show him the meaning of fear.

Shane became a man. As he leaned over Dr. Elihu, a drop of blood spattered down, staining the doctor's white coat. Shane glanced down at himself.

The impact hadn't been from a dart gun. He'd been shot in the chest. The wound wasn't bleeding much, and he didn't feel any pain. Yet.

Shane pressed the heel of his hand to his chest, sealing the wound. He'd worry about that later. Right now, he had some long-unfinished business to settle.

"*You're* the ultimate predator," Shane said. "You prey on people. You catch them. Kill them. Ruin their lives. I want you to know what it feels like to be on the other side. To be prey."

Shane looked into Dr. Elihu's eyes, and summoned his predator.

*I stalk. I kill. I lurk unseen.*

The doctor's sneer slipped away. His eyes widened with terror. The blood drained out of his face, leaving him an unpleasant pasty color.

*I am the teeth at your throat. I am the gun to your head. I am the blade in your heart.*

Dr. Elihu struggled frantically.

*Nothing can stop me. Nowhere is safe from me. No one can save you.*

The doctor thrashed so hard that he banged his own head against the floor. But he was no match for Shane's strength, nor could he break eye contact.

*I am the panther in the trees. I am the shark beneath the waves. I am the man with a knife.*

The doctor began to scream.

*I am the death you see coming. I am the fear in the dark. I am the night-mare turned real.*

Dr. Elihu's shriek of terror rose to an ear-piercing pitch, then suddenly stopped. His eyes rolled back in his head, and his entire body went limp.

Shane blinked in surprise. He'd scared the hell out a lot of people, but nobody had ever actually passed out before.

He got off Dr. Elihu, sat down on the floor, and took a second look. The doctor's chest wasn't moving. Shane touched the side of his throat. He had no pulse.

"I scared him *to death*," Shane said aloud. "I didn't even know I could do that."

"Serves him right." Catalina stepped up from behind him. "Shane, are you hurt?"

Whether it was the gunshot wound or the intensity with which he'd used his power or both, he suddenly felt shaky and weak. He could feel the bullet inside his body, jammed against one of his ribs like a burning coal.

"Yeah," Shane said. "He shot me."

"Oh, God." Catalina's hand closed convulsively over his shoulder. "I couldn't see from behind."

Shane covered her hand with his, trying to reassure her. He'd completely lost it when he'd thought she was dying. It was much easier to be on the other side. "Don't be scared. I have shifter healing."

Catalina took a few deep breaths, then regained her paramedic cool. "Sit tight and keep pressure on it. I saw a sign a little way back that said emergency supplies. I'll fetch a medical kit. It'll take two minutes, tops."

"Wait!" Shane hated the idea of her going into danger alone, even for a minute or two.

He forced himself to his feet. Everything went black around the edges. Next thing he knew, he was kneeling on the floor again.

"Shane!" Catalina was clutching his shoulders.

His vision cleared. "I'll be fine. Right here."

Catalina frowned anxiously, glancing from him to the direction of the emergency supplies and back. "Now I'm scared to leave you alone."

"Shifter healing, remember?" Shane put some force into his voice. "Just pass me Dr. Elihu's gun."

With a last worried look, Catalina handed it to him, then took off. With her astonishing new speed, she was out of sight in the blink of an eye.

"Keep a look-out," he called after her, but his voice didn't come out as loudly as he'd expected. His vision kept slipping ever so slightly out of focus. The gun, a lightweight Glock 22, felt heavy. He couldn't stop shivering.

*Shock,* he thought. *Internal bleeding. Stabilize the patient on-scene, then medevac immediately.*

His mate could handle the stabilization, but medevac was another story. The base could be fifty miles from anywhere. Shifter healing alone would keep him alive for a few more hours, no problem. But not for a few more *days.*

Catalina returned with a medical kit, plus an armful of clothing she must have taken off the tranquilized security guard they'd left outside of the lab. Or maybe she'd tranquilized a different guard she'd happened to come across on her way to the kit.

"Lie down," she said.

She put her arm behind his back and cupped his neck and head in her hands. Shane wasn't so far gone as to need help lying down, but he let her ease him to the floor. Her hands were warm against his bare skin, and he felt colder than ever when she slid them out from under him.

"Keep your back to the wall," he reminded her. Enemies could appear at any second. He was surprised they hadn't already.

"Oh, right." Catalina moved as he directed. She re-checked his breathing and pulse, then opened the kit and took out an airtight dressing.

He admired her professional deftness as she moved his hand aside and instantly applied the dressing, then neatly taped it down. "Good work."

"It better be." She touched his cheek. "You're freezing. You need to get warmed up. Here, have some clothes from a guy who's going to wake up cold and very confused."

Catalina started to slide her arm under his back.

"I can—" Shane began, then found that in fact, he couldn't sit up unaided. "This better not be a repeat of how we met."

Catalina helped him sit up and lean against the wall. He managed to haul on the guard's shirt and pants himself, but the effort left him alarmingly breathless.

"Just give me a second," he muttered.

She kissed him, the brush of her lips feather-light. "You saved my life. If you hadn't jumped him, I'd be the one with a bullet in my chest."

*A bullet in your head,* Shane thought. Dr. Elihu hadn't had time to shift his aim, and Catalina was much shorter than him.

With absolute sincerity, he said, "I'm glad I had the chance."

The stillness was broken by a series of distant shouts, gunshots, and running footsteps. Shane didn't waste his energy trying to get up. He could shoot perfectly well sitting down. Catalina crouched, ready to pounce, as Shane leveled his gun at the approaching enemies.

A familiar deep voice shouted, "Hold fire!"

"Hal?" Shane said incredulously.

The door at the end of the hall flew open as if it had been kicked. Hal stood in the doorway, nearly filling it with his burly frame. His brown hair brushed the frame as he ducked to step through without hitting his head.

He was followed by two more members of Shane's team from Protection, Inc. Destiny came first, holding a big gun in each of her small brown hands. Nick followed. His shirt was ripped halfway off his back, exposing his werewolf gang tats.

Despite his physical chill, Shane felt warm inside. His team had come for him. He'd hoped they would— he'd believed that they'd *try*— but on some level, he hadn't expected the cavalry to come. But here they were, shooting up a secret government base to rescue him.

"Hal *Brennan?*" Catalina said, a startled grin spreading across her face.

Hal and Nick came forward to crouch beside Shane. Destiny hung back, guarding the door. All of them spoke at once.

"Are you all right, Shane?" Destiny called, still watching the door.

"You look *fucked up,*" Nick pronounced, inspecting him. "What's the matter with you?"

"You're hurt," said Hal. "Where?"

"Bullet in the chest," Shane said. Identical expressions of alarm flashed across the very dissimilar faces of Hal, Nick, and Destiny. Hastily, Shane added, "I'm fine. Catalina treated me."

"Whoa, *no,*" Catalina interrupted. Speaking to Hal more than to Shane, she said, "He is not remotely fine. I did some emergency first aid, but he needs an ER."

Shane shook his head. "I can't go to an ER."

"You don't have to," Hal said. To Catalina, he explained, "We're not too far from my hometown. There's a doctor there who can take care of him."

Catalina visibly relaxed. "Oh, the one who had him on life support. Yeah, that should be fine."

"He told you about that?" Hal asked.

"When did you need life support?" Nick demanded. His green eyes fixed on Shane, intense and angry. "You never told us this place existed. Why didn't you ever fucking mention that there was an entire fucking black ops agency gunning for you?"

"Nick," Hal said. "Later."

"How did you find us?" Catalina asked.

"That's what we do," Shane said, at the same time that Hal replied, "Tracking, research, detective work. The usual."

Shane went on, "Where's the rest of the team?"

"Rafa, Fiona, and Lucas are on the other side of the building," Hal said in his rumbling voice. "They created a very large distraction so we could get to you, and they're about to create another."

"Did you see Justin?" Shane asked.

"Who's that?" Hal replied.

Catalina saved Shane the breath of attempting to summarize that whole story. "He has black hair and eyes. Pale skin. He was wearing jeans and a T-shirt."

The team looked at each other and shook their heads.

"We've only seen guards and medical people," Destiny said. "No one like that."

An explosion shook the building. Plaster dust drifted down.

"That's our cue," said Hal. "I'll carry Shane."

"Just help me walk. I don't want to tie up your gun-hand. Or mine." Shane didn't care how badly he was wounded or how shaky he felt. As long as he could hold a gun, he'd defend his mate and his team.

Hal helped Shane stand. Even that small movement dizzied him. The pain in his chest increased, threatening to double him over. Shane gritted his teeth and held tight to his gun, but his hands were shaking. He'd never be able to hit anything.

Destiny raised her arm in a signal. "We're clear! Come on!"

They went through the door. Shane could barely feel his feet touching the floor. Catalina's eyes were on nothing but him, her soft lips tight and narrow with concern. He was about to warn her to forget about him and watch for enemies when about fifteen guards burst out of closed doors.

Their enemies closed in on all sides in a final ambush. Destiny and Nick moved efficiently to cover each other and return fire. Hal fired at the guards, his trained arm moving steadily from one to the next.

Catalina leaped across the room, tackling a burly guard. He went down under her predator strength. The two of them went flying across the room. Catalina twisted impossibly in mid-air, landed in a crouch atop him, and banged his head into the floor. He went limp. Without hesitation, she jumped up and lunged to the side, knocking the weapon from another enemy's grip with a lightning-fast swat of her hand.

Shane could do nothing but observe his mate's agility and courage. His gun felt too heavy to lift. His *body* felt too heavy to lift. He could barely summon the strength to hold himself upright, let alone fight.

An explosion sent dust and bits of the ceiling showering down on their heads. Everyone staggered. Catalina, who had been mid-jump at the time, collided with a guard who had stumbled into her path. They both went down hard.

Catalina scrambled to her feet, blinking as if the impact had dazed her. The enemy she'd slammed into lay still. But another guard whipped around, swinging his pistol to bear on her.

Shane's gun hand had never been so steady. He fired, dropping the man aiming at his mate.

*Think of your weapon as an extension of your hand.* His long-ago drill instructor's voice echoed in Shane's ears. *Then you'll never drop it.*

The gun slipped from his fingers and clattered to the floor.

Next thing he knew, he was lying across Hal's shoulders. The team was running up a flight of stairs. Catalina ran beside them, clutching Shane's hand. He was infinitely relieved to see that she was unhurt.

Destiny kicked open a door. A cold, clear mountain breeze ruffled Shane's hair. The sky was the pale gray of pre-dawn. They ran outside and into the forest, not looking back. Then the loudest explosion of all echoed in Shane's ears. Hal and his team slowed as if that had been the signal they'd been waiting for.

"Fiona set charges," Hal said. "Apex won't be coming after you any more. Or anyone."

Fiona was very careful, Shane knew. So was everyone on their team. They would never set explosives without checking for bystanders first. Justin must have already made it out.

They came to Hal's car, parked off-road under a clump of pine trees.

"All clear!" a man called. "Clear by you?"

Shane recognized the voice as that of Ellie's brother, a Recon Marine. Ethan stepped out from where he'd been concealing himself, guarding the car.

"Clear by us!" Hal shouted.

Catalina stared at Ethan. "What are you doing here? You're not on the team."

"I was on leave," he said with a shrug. "Someone had to stay with the car to guard Ellie. She came in case anyone got hurt."

Hal's mate Ellie jumped out of the car, holding a medical kit.

"What happened to Shane?" Ellie asked, then broke off with a delighted gasp of, "Catalina!"

"Put me down," Shane demanded.

Hal tried to lay him on his back. Shane grabbed his arm and used it to haul himself up until he could sit up with his back against a tree.

Ethan turned to Hal, his military background evident in the crisp manner of his report. "Rafa, Lucas, and Fiona radioed in right before you got here. They'll be here in a few minutes." To Shane and Catalina, he said, "The team had planned to rescue you two and do as much damage as they could on the way. But Rafa said the lab was already destroyed when they got there."

Everyone looked at Shane. He turned toward Catalina. "My mate helped."

"Stop moving around." She put her hand on his chest, gently holding him in place. "You saved me. We won. We're *done.* You can relax now."

Catalina and Ellie began to examine him. He could see their long partnership in the smooth way they worked together, often without having to exchange a word. It was like the way the Protection, Inc. team worked. Or…

A flicker of movement caught Shane's eye. Justin stepped out of the forest. Instantly, the team and Ethan moved protectively between Shane, Ellie, and Catalina, their guns drawn.

"Friend!" Shane said. "Lower your weapons!"

Justin came forward as the team stepped aside, allowing him to pass. He crouched down beside Shane, examining him with a medic's practiced eye.

"Forgot to duck?" That sounded more like the old Justin.

"Come with us," Shane said. "I have to tell you—"

But Justin was shaking his head. "I can't. I'm supposed to be dead. I'll make trouble for you. You need help, right now, no interferences. I only came back to make sure you were all right. You're safer without me."

"No! I never had a chance— I never told you— " Shane spoke too quickly, leaving him coughing and breathless. He forced the words out. "They lied to you. I did do the ultimate predator process. I did need the treatments. There's a cure— I can take you—"

He couldn't get enough air to go on. Bright specks floated before his eyes.

"Easy." Justin laid a hand on his shoulder. "Tell me later. You need to get to a hospital now. I don't want to delay that. You're in good hands, right? You trust the people you're with?"

Shane managed a nod.

"We'll take care of him," Catalina said. "Ellie and I are paramedics, and we're taking him to a shifter doctor."

"Good." Justin squeezed his shoulder, then stood up and stepped back. Before Shane could stop him, he vanished into the forest.

Shane struggled to get up and go after him, but a heavy weight pressed down on his chest. Something must have fallen on him— maybe he'd been caught in an explosion. He could see movement all around him, but could make no sense of it. People were shouting, but he couldn't catch the words.

*Breathe,* hissed his panther.

That, he understood. Shane focused on his breathing as everything else faded away.

When he next opened his eyes, he was in the back seat of a moving car, lying with his head in Catalina's lap. His chest hurt. He instinctively moved his hand toward the pain.

Catalina caught it before he could complete the movement. "Are you back with us?"

He nodded. As his focus returned, he took in more of the scene. His legs rested across Ellie's lap. Hal was driving on a twisting mountain road.

"We didn't give you much for the pain," Ellie said apologetically.

Shane wasn't surprised. He had a gunshot wound and they were transporting him in the back of a car. Since they didn't have any electronic monitors, Shane needed to be able to notice and inform them if the pain suddenly got worse. It might be their only chance of treating a complication before it was too late.

"You see, if it suddenly starts to hurt a lot more," Ellie began.

"He knows, Ellie," Catalina interrupted, but not rudely. "He used to be a PJ."

Ellie looked down at Shane in surprise. "You never told me that."

*You have a lot of explaining to do,* his panther remarked.

Ellie leaned forward and poked Hal in the shoulder. "*You* never told me that. And I bet you knew."

"It was Shane's secret," Hal replied.

Shane suddenly realized that he'd never told Justin how he'd survived running away. If Justin didn't have any doctors he trusted…

Catalina squeezed his hand, catching his attention. "If you're worrying about Justin… You were right, he should have come with us. You're a panther and Hal's a bear and I'm a superhero and Ellie's got a gun, of course we could handle anything! But you did tell him that you had a cure. And I don't know if you noticed, but when he touched your shoulder, he put his hand right where your shirt was ripped. He has to touch your skin to track you. He was making sure he could find you when he needs you."

Her logic made sense. Shane was relieved that she'd known what he was thinking.

*Of course she does,* his panther hissed, exasperation audible in every rasping word. *She's your mate.*

Shane gazed past Hal's broad back and out through the windshield at the brightening sky, the occasional flake of snow drifting by, and the streaky granite cliffs. Hal was driving much faster than would normally be safe on these roads, but Shane trusted him not to go off a cliff.

Hal glanced into the rear-view mirror, his hazel eyes meeting Shane's in reflection. "Everyone's safe. They're driving separately. Except Lucas. He's flying."

Hal too had known what Shane was thinking without him having to ask. Shane nodded again. Even a single word felt like it would require strength that he might need for something more important later.

Catalina stroked his hair with a steady touch, as if she was petting a cat. If it hadn't been for the pain, his panther would have purred.

"Hang in there," Catalina said. "It won't be long now."

Shane relaxed into her caress. Like he'd told Justin, he was in good hands.

# CHAPTER FOURTEEN

## *Catalina*

Catalina hurried to Shane's bedside and bent over him anxiously. He'd been in surgery for a much shorter time than she'd expected and Dr. Bedford had assured her that he'd make a complete recovery. The monitors assured her that his vital signs were good and stable. But it was still frightening to see him lying unconscious and pale, his intense eyes closed.

Her leopard's purring voice sounded within her. *Your mate needs you. Lick his wounds and make him better.*

Catalina hoped her leopard didn't mean that literally. But the big cat was right that Shane needed her touch. She reached out to stroke his hair.

"You might not want to get that close," said a deep voice.

She turned around. Hal was standing in the doorway, with Ellie right beside him.

Ellie started forward, but Hal waved her back. "Wait in the lobby, Ellie. The team will be here any minute now. Don't let them come in till I give the go-ahead."

Ellie's eyebrows flew upward. "You think I can stop them?"

"I think you've got a better chance than Dr. Bedford," Hal replied.

"I'll do my best." Ellie went out, closing the door behind her.

Hal turned to Catalina. "Like I said. You'd better step back. Let me handle this."

Catalina shook her head. "No. He'll want me close when he wakes up."

"Shane's panther isn't like my bear," Hal said. "It can take control of him. And this is exactly the sort of situation that makes it go berserk. Just back off to the other side of the room, and stay there until I say it's safe."

Hal had seemed friendly before, but his rugged features were grim as he stepped forward. He loomed over her, taller than Shane and twice as burly. His size, which had been reassuring when they'd been fighting side by side, now seemed menacing.

*Stay with your mate,* her leopard hissed, but Catalina didn't need any prompting.

She wrapped a protective arm around Shane's chest. "Shane's my mate. He won't hurt me, and neither will his panther. *You* back off. I'm not going anywhere!"

A startlingly sweet smile softened Hal's face. He stepped out of Catalina's personal space, and walked around to settle down into a chair on the other side of Shane's bed. "Good. But keep an eye on him. He really might lash out when he wakes up."

She stared at Hal, puzzled by the instant shift from threat to approval. "Were you deliberately trying to scare me away from him?"

"I was trying to see if it was possible to scare you away," Hal replied.

"Why?"

Hal gave an embarrassed shrug. "Ellie's going to kill me when she hears about this. But Shane's been through a lot. I had to make sure you'd stand by him, no matter what."

"Oh," Catalina said, enlightened. "You were testing me to see if I was good enough for your buddy. Forget Ellie, *Shane's* going to kill you when he wakes up."

"Probably," Hal admitted. "And speaking of testing, I should warn you—"

Shane woke abruptly. The monitors all beeped their alarms, but it was drowned out by his snarl. His eyes were wide open but unfocused, his features twisted in the feral rage of a wild beast.

Catalina caught the hand that whipped up to try to yank the oxygen tube off his face. With her other hand, she stroked his hair. "Easy, Shane. You're safe. I'm right here with you."

He jerked his head to stare at her, then relaxed. The panic and fury faded from his gaze, leaving only the usual intensity of the man she loved.

"Sorry." Shane's voice was hoarse but calm.

Catalina had seen enough people wake up after surgery to know how dry the tube made your throat. "Want some water?"

He nodded. She helped him hold the glass steady as he drank through a straw. By the time he finished it, she could hear voices from outside the room, though she couldn't make out the words.

"The team's here," said Hal. "Can I let them in? They'll want to see you."

Shane glanced down at himself. Catalina tried to see through his eyes: the wires clipped to his chest, the bandages, the oxygen, the IV, the machines. Lying flat on his back in a hospital bed. The post-surgery weakness that had made his hands shake just trying to hold a glass of water. He must hate feeling so defenseless and exposed, when he was normally so cool and combat-ready.

"No," Shane said. "Not yet."

His eyes took on a familiar inward-looking gaze. Now that she had a leopard, she knew his panther was talking to him.

"What's he saying?" Catalina asked.

"He's telling me to let my pack in. Weird cat. Panthers don't have packs." Then, looking exasperated, Shane added, "And nobody's going to lick me."

Catalina giggled. "I think your panther and my leopard are on the same page."

"The team can visit later," Shane said. Pitching his voice so low that only she could hear, he said, "I don't want them to see me like this."

Catalina also spoke softly, but said, "Shane, the rest of the team showed up just in time to see you pass out. It looked like you were about to stop breathing. Ellie and I got you stabilized, and then we loaded you into Hal's car and burned rubber out of there. The team has got to be worried sick about you. Nobody cares what you look like. They just want to make sure you're all right."

"Let them in," Hal said. "Do it as a favor to me. I asked Ellie to hold them off, but she's way outnumbered."

"So am I," muttered Shane. Then he surrendered. "Fine. They can come in. Just let me sit up first."

He struggled to sit up, but even with Catalina's help, he was hampered by a rat's nest of medical tubes and wires. They were everywhere, attached to his chest, his elbows, his wrists, even the tips of his fingers. While he was still trying to disentangle himself, Hal hit a button, raising the head of the bed until Shane was sitting up. Then Hal went to let the team in.

They piled in, along with Ellie and Ethan. Catalina looked at the team members curiously as they all came in. Hal was the only one she'd had an actual conversation with, though she'd briefly met Nick and Destiny. When the other three had shown up, Catalina had been so busy giving Shane oxygen and monitoring his breathing that she'd barely even glanced at them.

She checked Shane to make sure he really was all right with having everyone there. But once he'd gotten past his first reluctance, he seemed pleased to see them. She was glad to see that they didn't crowd him, which she was sure he wouldn't like, but instead stepped up one at a time.

A blonde woman came forward first. Her platinum hair was braided and pinned to her head like a crown, and she made black fatigues look elegant. "Good to see you breathing. I thought I was about to lose my best sparring partner."

Shane shook his head, a half-smile hovering over his lips. Catalina could see that he and the blonde woman had the same easy camaraderie that he'd had with Justin. "I wouldn't do that to you, Fiona. Someone's got to keep you on your toes."

Fiona's sharp gaze raked over Catalina. Her eyes were green as emeralds, beautiful but cold. "Where were you when Shane was taking a bullet to the chest?"

It sounded like an accusation. Like she'd failed to protect him. Catalina wanted to defend herself, but there was truth in what Fiona had suggested. Meeting the woman's gaze squarely, Catalina said, "I'd run ahead of him. I was excited and I wasn't paying attention. He was hit protecting me."

"Cut her some slack, Fiona," Shane said. "It was her first time in combat. Don't tell me your first time was perfect."

To Catalina's surprise, the poised woman flushed pink. "You know it wasn't." Then, turning to Catalina, she said in a more friendly tone,

"You're honest. That's good. Maybe Shane will take some lessons from you."

"You should talk," Shane replied. But he sounded more amused than annoyed.

Catalina could see that Ellie was trying to signal to her from across the room. But Catalina didn't want to leave Shane's side if his teammates were all going to call him out for the secrets he'd kept from them.

Ethan stood beside Ellie, making their similarities more visible than ever. Though he was muscular where she was curvy, they had the same dark blonde hair, the same blue-green eyes, and the same snub nose. Catalina could even see some of the same freckles on Ethan's arms as he folded them across his chest, though most were obscured by his tattoos. He shot a glance at Catalina, then at Shane, and Catalina could see that he was trying to figure out whether he should defend one of them or both of them, or if interfering would make it worse. He glanced at Ellie, who shook her head and jerked her open hand at him, gesturing, *stay out of it.*

Sure enough, a handsome Latino man walked up, settled down on the edge of Shane's bed as if he was relaxing on his own sofa at home, and said, "So you're a PJ, huh? Well… That's not bad if you can't get through BUD/S. Seriously, it's a great second choice."

This time Shane did look irritated. "I never wanted to be a Navy SEAL, Rafa. I wanted to be the person who bails out the SEALs when they get in over their heads. And BUD/S is tough but it only lasts six months. The Pipeline takes two *years.*"

Rafa promptly replied, "That's because you're slow learners."

Catalina wanted to take Shane's side, but she couldn't help laughing at that. She regretted it immediately when Rafa turned to her.

"So, Catalina the cat lady. *How* many do you have?" Rafa's tone suggested that she was some elderly virgin who had scratching posts instead of furniture.

Doing her absolute best to keep a straight face, Catalina said, "Nineteen. Well— could be more now. Fluffy was pregnant when I left."

For a fraction of a second, she saw that Rafa believed her. Then he burst out laughing. "Well-played."

As the next team member approached, Catalina resigned herself to running the gauntlet of the entire Protection, Inc. team. But one glance at Shane showed that *he* wasn't resigned. His expression hardened as a young man with golden hair and chiseled features stepped up.

By process of elimination, that had to be Lucas. Lucas, the dragon shifter. Catalina stared at him. Like the rest of the team, Lucas wore simple black fatigues, but unlike the rest, his appeared to be tailored. His eyes, which she'd first thought were light brown, looked almost gold. And was that really a gold chain wrapped around his throat? Who wore jewelry into combat?

Lucas stared at Shane, then shook his head as if nothing he could say could possibly express how disappointed he was. Then he turned to Catalina. She braced herself for some cutting or snobbish remark— the guy was obviously wealthy and could probably spot her dirt-poor origins from a mile away— but instead, he said, "It's unfortunate that Shane can't test you himself. It's very revealing of character. But since he's too weak and helpless right now…"

Lucas paused deliberately, letting that jab sink in. Shane looked like he wanted to kill him. But before he could say anything, Lucas went on, "My people have our own ways of doing such things."

The golden shade of his eyes deepened and brightened, turning almost metallic. His sharp features shifted subtly, becoming less aristocratic and more strange. Almost… inhuman. He opened his mouth and let out a terrifying, reptilian hiss.

The sound went straight to some primitive part of Catalina's brain. She could almost see the shadow of vast wings, hear the roar of devouring flames. Instinctively, Catalina threw herself between Shane and the dragon.

Shane shoved himself forward, dislodging several wires. His heart monitor, which no longer registered a heartbeat, blared an alarm.

The glow in Lucas's eyes faded, and his features relaxed. He once again looked like an aristocrat masquerading as a bodyguard, not a monster posing as a man. Feeling foolish, Catalina stepped aside and turned off the alarm.

In the silence that fell, Shane turned slowly to lock gazes with his teammates, fixing them one by one with his predator stare. "That is enough! Catalina's my mate. I love her, and I trust her with my life. Anyone who has a problem with her had better go through me first."

"It's fine, Shane," Catalina assured him. "I think they were just trying to look out for you."

Destiny burst out laughing. "He knows that, Catalina. He did the exact same thing to Ellie and to Journey, Lucas's mate. Shane is just as overprotective as the rest of this macho crew." With a toss of her many braids, she added, "Of course, truly confident people have faith in their teammates' judgment and don't haze their mates."

"You're going to eat those words some day, Destiny," said Rafa.

Destiny gave a disbelieving snort. "Pffft! Not likely!"

Shane gave Nick a warning stare. "And you. Don't even think of it."

Nick shrugged. "I saw her fight. I got nothing to say." Then he rounded on Shane, a spark of anger in his green eyes. "To *her.* I've got lots to say to *you*. What do you think a pack— I mean a team— is for, if it's not to protect each other?"

As Nick began to stalk toward Shane's bed, Hal grabbed his shoulder and yanked him back. "I said later, and I meant later. Have it out with him once he's back on his feet."

"You *still* look fucked up," Nick muttered to Shane, but said no more.

Catalina, who had also moved to protect her mate, relaxed. Hal was looking out for him too. So was everyone. Even Nick, in his own way.

Ellie came up to pat Catalina's shoulder. "Sorry you missed my signal. I was trying to warn you about the hazing. Oh, well. You survived. So did I. At least I got the one man here who doesn't do that."

Hal caught Catalina's gaze from across the room. He might as well have had one of Catalina's own neon signs over his head, reading, DON'T TELL ELLIE I HAZED YOU TOO.

Catalina said nothing, but did her best to project, I WON'T BUT I MIGHT BLACKMAIL YOU WITH IT SOME DAY.

Hal hastily averted his eyes. "All right, everyone. Shane needs to rest. Let's give him some space."

Hal ushered everyone out, leaving Catalina and Shane alone. Once the door closed, Shane leaned back, no longer trying to hide his exhaustion.

"You want to lie down?" Catalina asked.

Shane nodded.

Catalina hit the button, lowering the bed till he was once again flat on his back. "Are you in pain?"

"Not really. I'm tired, mostly. And…" His face tightened, as if he was battling with himself. "They did some pretty bad things to me in the lab at Apex." He made a small gesture with one hand, indicating the tangle of wires and tubes. "I know I need this. But it scares my panther. When I first woke up, I was really out of it. I remember feeling trapped, but I'm not sure… "

Catalina hastily reassured him. "You didn't lash out at me, Shane. You tried to pull your oxygen tube out, that's all. No matter how panicked your panther gets, he won't try to hurt me. Ask him."

Shane's gaze drifted out of focus for a moment, and then he nodded. "Yeah. He says you're right. He says he might hurt *me* by accident, but never you." Looking mildly embarrassed, he added, "And he says he feels bad and he wants you to pet him."

Catalina stifled a giggle, more at Shane's expression than at the request, and stroked his hair. "What about you? How do you feel?"

"I feel bad, too," he admitted. "But it's better when you're touching me. Come a little closer…" He glanced at the wires. "If you can."

"This is where super-agility comes in handy." All the same, it took quite a lot of wriggling before she could get close enough to hold him.

She nestled in beside him, feeling cold wires and smooth bandages and warm skin. Her mate was alive and safe in her arms. He'd nearly died for her. Not only that, but he'd done something that she suspected was far more difficult for him: he'd trusted her enough to let her see his vulnerability. He laid his head down on her shoulder, turned to breathe in the scent of her hair, and fell into a deep and peaceful sleep.

***

Shane had told Catalina about shifter healing, but it still amazed her to see how much better he was by the very next day. She stayed with him all day, but by evening he pointed out that he wasn't dying, his panther wasn't going to go berserk, he had plenty of company, and there was no need for her to stick to him like glue.

"Go have a girls' night out with Ellie," he suggested. "I know you can't wait to catch up."

That turned into an *all* the girls night out— including Journey, Lucas's mate, a curvy woman with bright red hair and a golden dragon pendent nestled into the hollow of her throat. Journey had rushed in just as Catalina was about to leave, apologizing for her late arrival and saying that she'd just flown in from the Sea of Stars.

Shane had no visible reaction to that bizarre statement, but then again, that was Shane. He was hard to faze.

"Don't slack off your practice just because I'm not around," he warned her.

"I'm not," she assured him. "I get up every morning and do an hour of kata on the beach."

Shane seemed pleased with that. "That's good. Very traditional. They still train on the beach in Okinawa, where karate was invented. You should go there some day."

"It's on my list," said Journey.

When the women arrived at the nearest bar, which was at the next town and a two-hour drive away, they found a quiet room at the back where they could talk without being overheard.

Catalina asked Journey, "Where did you say you'd come from?"

"The Sea of Stars," Journey repeated. "It's a beach on Vadhoo Island."

"Where's Vadhoo Island?" asked Destiny.

"In the Maldives."

"Where are the Maldives?" asked Ellie.

"Off the coast of south India. The water is full of glowing plankton, like blue fireflies. It's like swimming through a starry night."

"What were you doing there?" Catalina asked.

Journey shrugged. "I saw a picture. It looked pretty, so I decided to visit. Once Shane's better, I'm going back and taking Lucas with me. Dragons love sparkly things. And the night sky."

That hadn't exactly answered Catalina's question. "I meant—"

Destiny laughed. "Lucas used to be a prince, Catalina. He's independently wealthy. Journey can go anywhere she likes, any time she likes. First class."

"Or on dragonback," Fiona added.

"You should all travel with me some time. Lucas would treat you." Hastily, Journey added, "But not the Sea of Stars. That one is just for the two of us. But later… Maybe a chateau in France?"

"What about a trek in Nepal?" Destiny suggested. "We could rent some yaks to carry our luggage."

"Just what I want to do on my vacation, chivvy around a bunch of hairy, slobbering cow-things." Fiona gave a delicate shudder. "I vote for the chateau."

"You're a snow leopard," said Destiny. "You should love Nepal."

"If I'm going on vacation, I want it to be relaxing," Fiona said firmly. "If you don't want a chateau, what about a villa in Tuscany?"

While Destiny, Fiona, and Journey discussed vacation destinations, Ellie and Catalina clinked their glasses together. Catalina had a shot of tequila with salt and lime. Ellie had a glass of hard cider.

"To us," Catalina said. "Partners forever."

"To us," Ellie echoed. "Together again."

They drank. The tequila burned its way down Catalina's throat. "My first drink as a shifter. I wonder if it'll affect me differently now."

"Got me," Ellie said. "Ask Fiona or Destiny— No, Destiny was born a shifter. She wouldn't know the difference. I'm not sure about Fiona. She doesn't talk much about her past."

"She still might not know. I'm not just a shifter, I'm a superhero. Shane's the only one who knows what that's like."

"Somehow I doubt that Shane thinks he's a superhero," Ellie remarked.

Catalina grinned. "He is, though. And so am I."

"What are you going to do with your powers?" Ellie asked. "I mean, there are definitely times when being super-strong would come in handy. No more calling for six orderlies to restrain the three hundred pound meth addict…"

"I'd still have to call for the orderlies," Catalina pointed out. "This has to stay secret. Apex may be gone, but I bet it's not the only place like it."

"That's true. The team's awfully careful about hiding what they are."

"But you're right," Catalina went on. "I've been thinking about it. I love being a paramedic, and I don't want to stop working with you. But I loved fighting with Shane, too. I know there's a lot I'd have to learn, but maybe I could join Protection, Inc. part-time. I could work with Shane in the day, and with you at night."

"When would you sleep?" Ellie asked.

"Sleep!" Catalina said with scorn. "Who needs it?"

She finished her shot and went to the bar to get another. When she returned, Ellie was still sipping her cider.

"So, you and Shane," Ellie said thoughtfully. "You know, I wouldn't have predicted it, but now that I've seen you together, it does seem right."

"I never could resist a cat," Catalina said with a laugh. Then, more seriously, she said, "You and Hal seem right together, too. You needed a man who respects you— who sees you as an equal. That's not easy to find."

"It's not," Ellie agreed. "Hal's a very special guy. And I don't just mean because he can turn into a bear."

Ellie glanced at the other three women, who were now arguing over which country had the best food, and spoke for Catalina's ears only. "We're talking about having a baby."

"Really?" Catalina was surprised for a moment. But when she thought about it, it felt as right as Ellie and Hal. Ellie's family had been torn apart by a bitter divorce. She'd always told Catalina that she'd never marry, let alone have a baby, unless she was certain that she wouldn't repeat her parents' mistakes. "No, I get it. You're mates. You know you'll never stop loving each other."

"It's not just that," Ellie said. "I want to keep working. I'll take a break, of course, but I love my job. I've never wanted to be a stay-at-home mom, but I don't want to leave my child with strangers, either. But if I had babysitters I trusted absolutely, who were like family, who'd protect my child with their lives…"

Catalina began to laugh. "You mean, like a team of shapeshifting, super-powered bodyguards?"

Ellie grinned. "Exactly. And if you count Hal and me and you— I can count you, right?"

"Of course you can," Catalina promised her. "Just so long as your baby isn't allergic to cats."

"Then that makes nine of us. Ten, when Ethan's around." With a slight wince, Ellie added, "Plus, there's Hal's family. His mother actually offered to move close enough to babysit if I gave her a grand-cub. I'm not sure how Hal would feel about that… Actually, I know how Hal would feel about that. But once she got her grand-cub, she'd have nothing to nag us about."

"Don't count on that," Catalina advised. "I don't know Hal's mom, but I can tell you that my grandma would just start nagging you to have another one."

Ellie finished her cider. "Oh, well. Guess we'll cross that bridge when we come to it. Besides, if I'm going to have one, I may as well have two. Everyone should have a brother or sister."

Catalina smiled to herself, trying to imagine Shane as a babysitter. Ellie's children might grow up playing horsie with a panther.

***

Catalina had already seen how quickly Shane could heal, but she was still amazed at how fast he recovered from his wound. By the next morning, he was restlessly pacing around the room until Dr. Bedford ordered him to lie down. Soon he was taking leisurely walks in the woods, and then less leisurely walks, and then Catalina caught him in the trees as a panther. But the team stayed with him until he had completely recuperated.

"See you back at the office," Destiny called as she, Rafa, Nick, and Fiona piled into a car. They drove off with a squeal of tires; Nick was at the wheel.

A cloud of glittering sparks gathered around Lucas. They whirled like a tornado, thickening until he vanished from sight. Then they winked out, and a golden dragon crouched where the man had been.

Journey climbed on to his back and waved. "We're off to the Sea of Stars!"

As Catalina stood gaping in amazement, the dragon leaped into the air. He flew higher and higher until he and his rider vanished into the clouds.

Ellie, Ethan, Hal, Shane, and Catalina were left alone together. Ellie, Ethan, and Hal had loaded their luggage into Hal's car, but Shane and Catalina had already decided to stay a while longer.

"Any idea when I should expect you back?" Hal asked.

"I'll let you know as soon as I do," Shane replied. "But I have to wait for Justin. I have a feeling he won't come looking for me until the last minute. If I have to transport him all the way from Santa Martina, he might not make it."

"Here." Hal tossed Shane a set of keys. "Stay at my cabin. It's not far. And it's a lot cozier than the hospital."

"Think of it as your honeymoon," Ellie suggested with a grin. "Hal and I have had a lot of fun there. By the way, the bed's an antique, but it's stronger than it looks. If Hal couldn't break it, you two don't need to worry. Go wild."

The faintest pink tinge spread across Hal's cheekbones. "Ellie…"

Shane didn't bat an eye. "Good to know."

# CHAPTER FIFTEEN

## *Shane*

Shane had never been to Hal's cabin before. It *was* cozy, isolated in the middle of the forest but equipped with nearly everything anyone could want in a vacation cabin, from extra clothes in all sizes to a well-stocked freezer to a spare car parked beneath a tree. Since it belonged to Hal's technophobic bear clan, it had no computer or even television, but did come with several cases of books. Shane supposed they were lucky to have the car. Hal told him that after he and Ellie had gotten stranded in the woods when they'd first met, he'd bought it for the cabin.

"I told my family it was in case of emergencies," Hal told Shane in his rumbling voice. "But you and Catalina help yourselves if you want anything from town."

Shane and Catalina enjoyed their stay. They played wild games in the forest, chasing each other through the tree-tops, sometimes as a panther and a leopard, sometimes as a big cat and a woman who climbed like one. Then they returned to the cabin to read and eat. Neither of them knew how to cook, unless you counted lobsters and MREs, so after a few days of charred disasters, they resorted to meals that Hal's mom, grandma, and uncle had cooked and then frozen. Shane didn't pay much attention to what he ate, but Catalina always happily remarked how much better it was than the packaged frozen meals she usually lived on.

The rest of the time they spent making love in the bed, which was just as sturdy as Ellie had promised. Also in the shower, on the sofa, on the floor, and in the forest. Shane hadn't forgotten his promise to keep it exciting for Catalina, but whether they were having passionate sex up against a tree or sleepy lovemaking first thing in the morning, it was thrilling whether he made a special effort or not. Every moment, every kiss, every touch was as sexy and heart-stopping as their very first time. They couldn't get enough of each other.

They'd been at the cabin for a week when Shane awoke from a deep sleep to the sound of stumbling footsteps, unmistakable as those of someone forcing themselves forward on willpower alone. He was out of bed and yanking the front door open before it even occurred to him that it could be an ambush.

Justin stood swaying in the doorway, one hand bracing himself against the frame, the other still upraised to knock. The sight of that familiar face with those strange near-black eyes and dark hair once again gave Shane a shock of unsettled recognition. Justin's skin was white as bone in the moonlight.

"Comeback?" Justin's voice was alarmingly weak. "I'm sick. I need help."

"Any time, Red." Shane put a hand on his shoulder, steadying him. "You don't even need to ask."

"I know."

Shane caught him as he collapsed. Justin was burning up, his shirt and skin damp with sweat, but he was shaking as if he was chilled. The air rasped in and out of his lungs, each breath sounding like it required a tremendous effort.

Shane carried Justin into the living room, where he laid him down on the couch. Catalina was already there, waiting in pajamas with the medical kit in her hand, as bright and alert as if it was the middle of her workday. In fact, Shane recalled, under normal circumstances it would be.

Catalina knelt beside the couch to check Justin's vital signs. Shane did too. Justin's breathing was labored and shallow, and his pulse was weak and rapid. He didn't respond to his name, or to a hard pinch on the back of his hand.

"He looks bad," Catalina said. "Load and go?"

Shane's chest tightened at her words. Justin did look bad. Non-responsive, signs of shock, high fever, respiratory distress… Every sign was critical, and no one knew better than Shane how easily even one of those could lead to cardiac arrest.

*Justin's a survivor,* Shane told himself. *He made it through the Pipeline. He's a ten-year combat veteran. He survived ultimate predator. He survived two years with Apex. And he made it here, on foot, from God knows where. He's not going to die on me now.*

"Yeah," Shane said. "You drive. If he wakes up disoriented, I've got a better chance at calming him down before his snow leopard takes over. We've had ten years' worth of trusting each other with our lives. He might remember even if he's delirious."

And if Justin's snow leopard did take over, Shane wanted himself between its claws and Catalina.

"I'll get the keys," she said. "And call Dr. Bedford to meet us in her office. We'll be on the road in five."

Shane was reassured by how calm and competent she was, not to mention willing to take off in the middle of the night and in her pajamas. She was not only his lover but his partner, someone he could trust absolutely and rely on to carry her own weight. She'd even carried *his* weight once. He was so lucky to have found her.

Justin's eyelids began to flutter. Caught between sleep and waking, conscious enough to feel pain but not conscious enough to hide it, he moaned and turned his head back and forth as if he was trying vainly to escape from his own body. Shane remembered that relentless stabbing pain, as if his bones had been replaced by broken glass.

*Lick his wounds,* his panther advised.

*Stop saying that,* Shane replied silently. *It's gross.*

He opened the medical kit and filled a syringe.

Justin moaned again, then opened his eyes. "What's that?"

He sounded dazed, so Shane kept it simple. "For the pain."

"I can stand it," Justin said immediately. Shane suspected that he was stripped down to a PJ's most basic instincts: show no weakness, find your friends, hunker down and endure.

"I know you can," Shane said. "But you don't have to."

Justin peered at the label on the tiny bottle. "What is it?"

Shane held it closer, though he doubted that Justin could focus enough to read the fine print. "It's just morphine. You've had it before, remember? I gave you some when you took a round to the chest."

"This hurts more," Justin admitted.

Shane knew how bad he had to be feeling to confess that. It was a mark of pride for military personnel to deny pain, which created another sort of pain— a pain in the ass— for medics. Back when he'd been a PJ, Shane often had to resort to asking, "Where do you feel *it?*" and "How bad is *it?*" to get any sort of useful answer out of his patients.

"I know." Shane pushed up Justin's sleeve and gave him the shot. "There, that should hold you till we get you to the doctor."

Catalina returned with a rolled-up blanket under one arm and a ring of keys jingling in her hand. "All set?"

Justin looked up at her, guilt deepening the lines of pain etched into his face. "I'm sorry. What I did to you—"

"Don't worry about it," Catalina interrupted him. "It's water under the bridge. And any buddy of my mate's is a buddy of mine."

"Thanks. Buy you a drink later." Justin's eyes widened in surprise, and then he seemed to melt into the couch as all his muscle tension released at once. "Oh. There we go."

Shane recognized that moment familiar to all medics, the shock of relief when unbearable pain suddenly eases. Released from the burden of long-borne suffering, patients often immediately fell asleep. Shane wasn't surprised when Justin's eyes closed.

"Justin?" Shane asked softly. After a moment, he tried, "Red?"

Justin didn't stir. Catalina crouched beside him as Shane rechecked his vital signs.

"You've seen this before— you've lived this. How is he, really?" Catalina asked. She put her arm around Shane.

His own tension released at her touch. "I know he looks bad. But he's in better shape than I was when Hal found me. I think Dr. Elihu was right— the longer you live with the process, the more your body adjusts and the easier it is to stop the treatments. Justin's been living with it for two years now."

All the same, he hurried to the car with Justin in his arms. Catalina ran ahead to unlock it and open the doors. Shane got Justin settled as comfortably as he could manage, lying across the back seat with his head in Shane's lap. Catalina draped the blanket over him and helped Shane give him oxygen. Then she took a flying dive into the driver's seat, starting the car before her butt even touched the seat.

"Show-off," he said.

"You love it," she immediately replied.

The exchange, which had become a joke between them, relieved some of his anxiety. As Catalina pulled out of the driveway, she reached back to lay her hand on Shane's shoulder. The position would have been uncomfortable for any normal person, but she made it look graceful and easy. Shane laid his hand over hers, holding it like a lifeline.

"How're *you* doing?" she asked.

"I'm fine," he began, then remembered not to lie to her. "I'm worried about him. But I'm glad he's back. And I'm glad you're here with me."

The mountain roads were very dark. The headlights' beam made trees loom up suddenly, then vanish into the black.

Catalina was an excellent driver, pushing the car as fast as it could safely go but maintaining an even speed so Justin wouldn't be jarred. Shane remembered that when she and Ellie had been partners as paramedics, Catalina had driven the ambulance while Ellie treated patients in the back.

"You went through this too," Catalina said. They were both speaking softly, as if they were afraid to wake Justin, though Shane knew he would wake on his own or not at all.

"Yeah." Shane touched his friend's forehead. His skin was far too hot, but the sweat welling up was icy. Shane remembered how it had felt as vividly as if it had happened yesterday instead of a year ago: the cold sweat, the burning fever, the sense of suffocation, the pain that made every movement an agony. "Now that I've been shot too, I can tell you that Justin was absolutely right. This hurts a hell of a lot more than a bullet in the chest. I didn't want to make a big deal of it in front of Hal, but you could've wrung out my shirt like a dishrag."

Catalina squeezed his hand. "I wish I could've been there for you."

"You were there when I needed you most. And I wasn't alone back then. I had Hal."

"Everything comes around," Catalina said. "Now Justin's got you."

As she drove through the night, Shane remembered how alone he'd felt when he'd collapsed in the woods, lying on a bed of autumn leaves and waiting to die. He'd had no hope of survival or redemption, of justice or revenge. The pain had been so bad, he couldn't even appreciate the last few moments of life he'd thought had been left to him. What little strength remained to him had been spent on hoping it would all be over soon.

But Hal had found him. And every time he'd been offered a chance to live, he'd taken it, even when he'd thought it was a forlorn hope. And all that agony had been worth it. His life hadn't been ruined, just changed. He'd lost the PJs, but he'd gained Protection, Inc.

*Your pack,* his panther hissed.

*Panthers still don't have packs,* Shane answered silently. *Weird cat.*

*Weird human,* his panther retorted. *Of course we do. You have one of your pack* in your lap. *And another one is driving the car.*

Shane had to admit that the big cat had a point. Justin had returned, and Shane could hear the unbreakable endurance of the PJ he'd been in his every labored breath. And Catalina was right there with him, pushing the car to its limits with one hand controlling the wheel with smooth confidence and one hand resting easily on his shoulder.

*My mate,* he thought. It was as much of a shock of wonderment now as when he'd first recognized her. It resonated all the way down to his heart.

"I have you," he said aloud.

"And I've got you," she replied as easily as if she'd heard the entire conversation. "I never thought I'd find a man whose idea of a perfect night out is transporting a critically ill patient at 3:00 AM. I guess it really is true that there's someone for everyone."

Catalina brought the car to a smooth stop in front of Dr. Bedford's office. Her Range Rover was in the otherwise empty lot, and the lights were on. They glowed warm and welcoming. She was the only doctor Shane had ever encountered who used normal lights, like you'd have in a house, instead of harsh white fluorescent strips.

Shane carried Justin inside. As Catalina closed the door behind them, Dr. Bedford gestured toward a hospital bed.

"Put him on that, please," she said.

Shane laid him down. Dr. Bedford began attaching electrodes to his chest. As she stuck one on, Justin awoke suddenly with a cry of pain. Eyes wild, teeth bared, he snarled at the woman in the white doctor's coat.

"Red!" Shane called to him, but Justin was beyond understanding.

An instant later, a snow leopard crouched on the bed. He let out a hair-raising howl of pain and rage, then sprang at the startled doctor.

Shane threw himself between them, tackling the snow leopard and throwing him to the ground. But Shane rolled at the last second, taking the impact on his own body. His friend was sick and in pain; the last thing he needed was to get slammed into the floor.

"Don't fight," Shane gasped. "It's Comeback, Red. I'm your friend!"

But he knew Justin didn't understand. *Justin* wasn't there; his snow leopard was in control, delirious with fever, overcome by pain, panicked at the sight of doctors and medical equipment, and desperate to escape. No doubt Justin had undergone his share of painful and unpleasant experiments at Dr. Elihu's hands.

The snow leopard lashed out, fighting to escape Shane's grip. Shane wrapped his arms and legs tight around the beast, burying his face in the leopard's neck to avoid its fangs. While they struggled on the floor, Shane heard Catalina and Dr. Bedford urgently conferring, but couldn't catch the words over the snarls and eerie shrieks of the snow leopard.

Then Catalina darted in with a syringe in her hand. With her incredible speed and agility, she jabbed it into the snow leopard's haunch, then sprang away before the beast could claw her.

Shane didn't dare relax physically, but he was immensely relieved. Any second now the big cat would collapse beneath him, deep in a tranquilized sleep…

The snow leopard shook itself violently, nearly throwing Shane across the room.

"It's not working," Dr. Bedford said, sounding surprised.

*Captain Obvious,* Shane thought.

"What was it?" Catalina asked. The leopard growled loudly enough to drown out the doctor's reply, but Catalina's clear voice carried through it. "He's immune to tranquilizers!"

Shane swore to himself. Catalina had mentioned that, but it had been before either of them had known who the mysterious shifter was. Obviously both she and Shane had completely forgotten that in the surprise of learning his identity.

"Try morphine!" Shane shouted, then ducked another swipe of those sharp claws.

He again wrestled the snow leopard into submission. The big cat was weak, fighting with the strength of desperation alone, or Shane would never have been able to handle him in his human form. But he managed to keep a grip on the snow leopard, though the big cat struggled fiercely beneath him.

Dr. Bedford handed Catalina another syringe. She darted in and neatly slipped it into the loose skin between the snow leopard's shoulders, then jumped back as the big cat nearly broke through Shane's hold.

"Stay clear," Shane called, forcing the animal down again. "Give it a minute to work."

He grimly pinned the snow leopard until its struggles eased off.

Hoping that Justin would understand him once he wasn't overwhelmed by pain and panic, Shane said, "Shift, Red. You need to be a man now."

A second later, Shane knelt beside a trembling, gasping man. Justin's bewildered gaze drifted around the room, then fixed on Shane.

"Comeback?" Justin's voice was startlingly strong and confident. It made an odd pang go through Shane. That was how his friend used to sound all the time. "You're bleeding. Let me get my kit. Some of those will need sutures."

"Sure," Shane said, after an instant's confused pause. "Get your kit, Red."

Justin relaxed at Shane's words. His eyes slid shut, and his breathing steadied.

"He's right," Catalina said, frowning at Shane. "You do need stitches. Dr. Bedford, can I borrow your supplies?"

"That cabinet." The doctor pointed to it. To Shane, she said, "If you don't mind…?"

Shane lifted Justin back on to the bed. As Dr. Bedford once again began to examine Justin, Shane reached down to re-check his pulse.

"Out of my way, please," said the doctor.

"But—"

A small hand came down on his shoulder.

"You heard her. Sit down." Catalina pushed him into a chair. "Doctor's on duty. Let her do her thing, and let me do my thing."

For the first time, Shane looked down at himself. He was bleeding from deep claw wounds on his arms and chest and thigh. Once he noticed them, they began to sting.

Catalina got the supplies from the cabinet and filled a syringe.

"No drugs." Shane couldn't afford to sleep when his mate might need him to defend her and his friend might need to be protected from himself.

"It's just a local anesthetic, to numb the area," she said. Then, with gentle irony, she added, "But I could stitch you up with nothing if you really want me to."

His wounds instantly hurt more as he imagined that. "Sorry. It's fine."

*Idiot,* his panther remarked. *Your mate isn't going to drug you. She knows you wouldn't want that. She knows because she's your mate. When are you going to get that into that thick head of yours?*

*Stop being right all the time,* Shane replied silently.

Catalina gave him several shots of local anesthetic, then cleaned and stitched his wounds. Her sutures were neat and small, better than his; he was used to working in combat conditions, focusing on saving lives and leaving anything that wasn't immediately life-threatening for someone else to deal with later. She'd obviously had far more practice with minor injuries. Even if he hadn't had shifter healing, she'd have ensured that he healed without scars.

Once she was done, he sat down in a chair by Justin's bed. Catalina sat beside him with her arm around his shoulders.

"Look, he's better already," she remarked.

Shane glanced from his friend's pale face to the monitors. Catalina was right; Justin was breathing more easily now, and his heart rate was down.

"So he can't be sedated, huh?" Dr. Bedford asked. "I'll keep him on a morphine drip. Hopefully he won't panic if he's not in pain. All the same... you'd better stay with him."

"Don't worry," Shane said. "I won't leave him."

And he didn't. Dr. Bedford moved another bed into the room so Shane and Catalina could take turns watching over Justin.

But Justin never again tried to transform or fight. When he woke, all Shane had to do was say, "You're sick, Red. You're in a hospital. I'm staying with you till you're better."

Often Justin would simply nod, then go back to sleep. Sometimes he asked about missions from years ago, or if his buddies were all right.

Shane could usually assure him with perfect honesty that everyone was fine. He'd kept tabs on all the PJs he'd known. But once Justin asked about Mason. Shane had no idea if Justin meant the mission they'd been on when Apex had captured them, or some other mission, or if he thought they were all still at Apex. But Shane couldn't lie about that.

"Mason didn't make it," Shane said. "I was there. It was quick. He didn't suffer."

"Oh," Justin sighed, and Shane saw that on some level Justin had already known. But he turned his head away, hiding his face in the pillow. Shane kept a hand on his shoulder until he slept again.

If Justin woke when Catalina was watching, she'd point to Shane and say, "Shane's right there. He's fine; he's just taking a nap. He's here to take care of you." That too seemed to satisfy him.

Shane had needed full life support for a week, and he'd still almost died. But Justin required nothing more than rest, oxygen, IV fluids, and medication to reduce his fever and support his heart and lungs. And from his reaction every time he awoke and saw Shane beside him, Shane suspected that the knowledge that he was finally free and with friends was also essential to his healing. If Hal hadn't stayed by Shane's side, Shane doubted that he'd have found the strength to survive.

Justin's fever broke in a few days, but he had no memory of anything after passing out on Hal's couch. Shane decided not to tell him the rest. He knew all too well how much Justin probably had to feel guilty about. He didn't need to know that he'd hurt Shane. By that time, his claw wounds had healed without a trace.

Once Justin was well enough to walk around, he sent Catalina and Shane out, telling them they must be going stir-crazy. When Shane said honestly that he wasn't, Justin bluntly informed him that he needed some time to himself.

Catalina went off to telephone Ellie. Shane took a hike in the forest. He didn't follow a trail and, by habit, didn't leave one either. But he wasn't surprised when he heard footsteps behind him, deliberately crunching twigs and leaves so as not to startle him. He knew who it was before he turned around.

Justin was out of his hospital pajamas and in the clothes he'd worn when he'd first shown up at the cabin: jeans, a T–shirt, and hiking boots. He was thinner and paler than he should be, but he stood strong and straight. But what surprised Shane was that he'd found a pair of scissors and clipped his hair close enough to get rid of the black. It was much shorter than he'd usually worn it, but once again bright as a new penny.

"Thanks for..." Justin shook his head as if there was too much to name. "For everything."

He didn't say *"Goodbye,"* but Shane heard it in his tone.

"Why don't you join Protection, Inc.?" Shane asked. "It's not quite parachuting into combat zones, but I think you'd like it. And you never know, some day there might be parachuting."

Justin didn't smile— Shane had never seen him smile since they'd been PJs together— but the skin around his strange black eyes crinkled like maybe he was thinking about smiling. "Did your boss authorize you to bring on new team members?"

"No," Shane replied. "If he has a problem with it, I'll just beat on him till he gives in."

Justin's eyes crinkled a little more, then smoothed out as he seemed to give Shane's suggestion some serious thought. "Maybe later. Not now. I've got some stuff I need to sort out on my own."

Shane wished he'd been willing to stay. But his friend was back, more-or-less from the dead, and that was the important thing. "Your call. Whatever you decide, you know where to find me."

Justin smiled. For the very first time, those dark eyes looked familiar. "Yeah. I can always find you now."

He walked into the woods. Shane stood watching the forest after he disappeared from sight. A few minutes later, a snow leopard stalked out from between the trees. He leaped onto an overhanging branch and stared at Shane with eyes green as pine needles, green as Justin's eyes used to be. Then he climbed away through the trees until the white of his coat was lost against the snow of the distant mountains.

Shane walked back to Dr. Bedford's office, wondering if Justin had told her he was leaving. He doubted it. Shane leaned against a towering redwood near the parking lot, trying to decide how much to tell her.

He felt a disturbance in the air, and turned to see that Catalina had come up beside him.

"I didn't hear you," he said. "Creeping up on little cat's feet."

She laughed and tipped her head back, inviting his kiss. Her lips were as warm and sweet as the first time, her body soft and responsive as it pressed against his.

"He's gone, isn't he?" Catalina asked.

"Yeah. I invited him to join Protection, Inc., but he said he had stuff he needed to do." Shane was less disappointed than he would have expected. It had taken him a year, a team, and finding his mate to come to terms with what had happened to him at Apex. He understood why Justin too needed time.

"Come home with me now," Catalina said, slipping her hand into his. "I want you to meet the family."

***

Shane spent the entire drive bracing himself to meet her family. If they didn't approve of a paramedic, they wouldn't approve of a bodyguard, even one who probably made better money than the average lawyer. But instead of the big family home she'd described, she pulled up at an apartment building.

Shane laughed. "Oh. *This* family."

Catalina grinned at him. "You can run the gauntlet of my relatives later. It'll be just like me meeting your team, except once they finish harassing you, they'll feed you to make up for it. I hope you like tamales."

"Love 'em."

"How about cats?"

"To eat?"

Catalina rolled her eyes at him, then punched him in the arm. She'd gotten more used to her power by then; it didn't hurt at all.

"I like cats," Shane said. "I don't know how they'll feel about me, though. I don't think I've met any since I became one myself."

"Then this should be interesting." Catalina unlocked the door.

Her apartment was small but cozy, lived-in but not cluttered. There was a comfy-looking sofa, photos of her family, a TV and video game console, and a bookcase mostly filled with video games and DVDs. An elaborate, multi-story cat house was in one corner.

Catalina crouched down, and Shane followed her. Catalina's family appeared to be lurking under the sofa.

He patted the floor. "Here, kitty, kitty."

Three sets of glowing eyes stared back at him. One cat spat loudly, one hissed, and a third darted out from under the couch and leaped into Catalina's arms.

"Poor baby," said Catalina, but she was laughing, too. She rubbed the black and white cat behind its ears. It purred, banging its head hard into her arm, then turned to Shane and let out an angry yowl. "Maybe give them time to get used to you?"

*They're jealous*, said Shane's panther with satisfaction. *Now they have to share.*

"Good idea," Shane said aloud. "Maybe they'll like me better if I stay in the bedroom for a while."

"By yourself," Catalina said, nodding. "Give me some quality alone time with them."

Shane put his hand on the small of her back and gave her a gentle shove. "Into the bedroom with you, woman."

Clutching the cat tight to her chest, she did a backflip across the room, out of his reach. The cat yowled again, but it sounded more excited than scared. Shane bet it was saying, *One of us!*

"*You* stay in the bedroom," Catalina retorted. "I wasn't kidding about the alone time. My kitties and I haven't seen each other in months! Don't forget, there was all that time I spent in Loredana."

Shane had forgotten about that. "Okay. Have your reunion. I'll entertain myself. I got lots of practice with that at Apex."

"It's on the left," Catalina called, over a chorus of happy meows.

Her bedroom was also small and cozy, but the bed was big enough for two. A backpack of emergency supplies was stashed under the bed, alongside a full duffel bag that Shane had no doubt was her go-bag, already packed with everything she'd need if she was called up to go abroad into a disaster zone on an hour's notice and with no idea how long she'd stay. He'd had one too when he'd been a PJ. He had one still, out of habit, even though his bodyguard assignments were never that rushed.

*Just how similar* are *we?* Shane wondered.

He felt along the bed until he found the dent where Catalina usually slept, then lay in it and reached out into the bed frame. His first try found nothing, but then he remembered that his arms were much longer than hers. When he felt in the place that would be within her arm's reach, he found a heavy flashlight, perfect for knocking out an intruder.

Catalina opened the door. Three cats skulked warily behind her, then drew back and hissed at the sight of Shane.

Shane held up the flashlight. "I found your weapon."

"It's actually in case there's an earthquake," she said, looking embarrassed.

"Catalina. It's exactly where I keep my gun."

"Okay, yeah, it's my weapon," she confessed. "I've never had to use it, but I like having it, just in case. I don't need it any more now, I guess. Still… If there was an earthquake…"

"Of course you should keep it." Shane replaced the heavy flashlight. "Who gave you a hard time about it?"

"A jerk who never got invited back again," she said. "He called me paranoid and said I'd never be able to fight off a man anyway. He'd have had a nice night with me if he'd just kept his mouth shut. We were already undressed. I picked up his clothes and threw them and him out the front door."

"I hope it was a cold night," Shane said.

Catalina smiled. "The next morning, I found footprints in the frost. Barefoot. I accidentally dropped his shoes on our way out."

She came into the room and beckoned to the cats. They hung back, staring balefully at Shane. He crouched down, trying to make himself seem less threatening. It didn't work. They backed away, their fur puffed up and their tails lashing.

"They hate me," Shane said.

"They'll get over it," replied Catalina.

*They bow before their proper lord and master,* hissed Shane's panther smugly.

*Don't be ridiculous*, Shane replied. *Cats don't have lords or masters. Not even housecats.*

"Did you show them your leopard?" Shane asked Catalina.

"I did! They were thrilled. I foresee lots of time with us all sleeping in a pile on the sofa. If my leopard fits on the sofa." She grinned at him. "Maybe I'll buy a giant deluxe couch so we can all fit. Your panther too."

That sounded pretty good to Shane. "What are their names?"

"The black one is Jessica Jones, the orange tabby is Natasha Romanova, and the black and white one is Rogue."

His mate's pets were all named after superheroines. Of course they were.

He offered the cats his hand. Jessica spat at him and ran away. Rogue gave him a cautious sniff. Natasha tilted her head, considered him silently with her brilliant green eyes, and then nudged his palm. When he petted her, she bit him and fled.

Shane wryly examined his bleeding hand. "We're going to need a demilitarized zone."

Catalina lifted his hand and kissed it. "That'll be the bedroom."

She kicked the door shut. It slammed behind her back, making the frame shake. The atmosphere in the room altered in an instant, switching from easy playfulness to a charged intensity.

Shane remembered how he'd showed her his kata in their prison at Apex. He'd known halfway through that this was the moment, this was how he'd lose control, this was when they'd kiss for the very first time. When she'd pressed herself against his hard-on, he'd known that he had to offer to step away, but he'd also known that she'd refuse. He'd known that in just seconds, they'd be making love, him inside her, her enveloping him, their bodies and hearts changing a place of cold and fear into one of heat and passion.

He could feel that same knowing urgency now. Catalina's breasts were heaving beneath her low-cut blouse, her breath loud enough to hear. They snatched at each other, falling hard against the door. The frame shook again, sending a vibration through their bodies.

He bent to kiss her, smelling the cinnamon spice of her hair as it fell across his face, cool against his burning skin. Then he bent lower, pressing his mouth into the delicious curve where her shoulder met her throat. He flicked his tongue across that soft flesh, tasting salt, feeling nothing but smooth skin. She was a shifter too now, quick to heal. The scar of his last bite was long since gone.

She gripped his upper arms, fingers digging in tight. The sensation was more intense than painful, though it was hard enough to bruise. He wondered if she knew, and meant to leave her marks on him. They'd be gone soon enough, but he liked the idea of having the imprint of her fingers on his body.

"Go on," she whispered. "I want you to."

He bit down, quick and hard, tasting copper. She gasped, her fingers tightening even harder, but he knew it was from excitement, not from pain. Or at least, not from the bad kind of pain. Even with his human senses, he could smell her arousal, hot and musky and very, very female. It had to be soaking through her panties.

His cock pressed up against her belly, rubbing into her soft flesh with every inhale and exhale of her breath. He didn't know how much more he could stand. His blood had been replaced with pure adrenaline. He couldn't control his breathing. He was shaking with desire, tremors running up and down his body like he was freezing to death. He had to get in from the cold.

Catalina licked a drop of sweat from the hollow of his throat. Her voice was a throaty purr as she said, "This is why I wore a skirt."

Shane had assumed she'd dressed more formally to see her family. The real explanation excited him so much that his hands shook as he unzipped his jeans. His cock had been so tight against the denim, releasing it was a tremendous relief. The sensitive head was slick and glistening, the shaft rock-hard and throbbing.

He reached under her skirt to pull off her panties. His fingers slipped between her slick thighs, then sank into wet heat. She wasn't wearing any panties.

A bolt of lightning shot up his spine. He heard himself groan, even as she gasped and thrust herself against his fingers. He wanted to be inside her so much, so much, *now*. But she was gasping in his ear, her face flushed, her eyes closed and her black eyelashes fluttering. Her hot juices ran down his hand, and he could feel her clit swell and pulse.

She was so close to coming, just from his fingers inside her, it was all he could do to not come himself, without even being touched. He buried his face in her shoulder, biting her again, marking her as his own, as she cried out her climax and her inner walls pulsed against his fingers.

"Shane..." she gasped. "Shane..."

"I— I have to—" He couldn't even get the words out. He grabbed her under the hips, lifted her off her feet, and pushed her up against the door.

His fingers were wet with her juices. He could smell her arousal, her own unique scent, as strongly as if he was going down on her. The taste of copper was in his mouth. He thrust into her, burying himself in that liquid heat. Now he was in her, as she was in him.

In the entire time they'd been making love, she'd never let go of his arms, not once. Her grip tightened to the point of pain as he thrust inside her, but that only made him more excited. Her smell, her tight wet heat, her soft gasps, her responsiveness to his every thrust, the contrast between her soft flesh and the iron grip of her fingers— all of it was driving him wild. They were two of a kind, halves of a whole, mates who needed to live on the edge, in the place where pain and pleasure met, where danger made you feel alive, where you and your beast were one.

Shane let go of control, abandoning himself to the wildness within him. And not only wildness, but pleasure and passion and freedom and love. His climax shattered his senses, then reknit him new and whole. He and Catalina were so close as to be one heart in two bodies, and yet he felt more himself than he had in years.

*Finding your mate is finding yourself*, he thought. *This is me. I'm finally back.*

He set Catalina down. She staggered, clutching at his arm for support. Shane didn't feel too steady himself. Luckily, the bed was right there beside them. They collapsed on it and lay together, gasping and sweaty and content.

Catalina gave a long sigh of pleasure and ran her fingers through his hair. "It's good to be home."

Shane knew she wasn't just talking about her apartment. *He* was her home, the place where she was loved and safe, respected and treasured. And she was his.

Her soft breasts pressed into Shane's chest, and her strong legs curled around his. He'd never felt such a sense of belonging in his life.

She ran her fingers around his upper arm, tracing the marks she'd left. Before Apex had taken and remade him, such new bruises would have been red. But with his accelerated healing, they were already black against his pale skin, the outlines of her fingers sharp as tattoos. By the next morning, they'd be gone, just like the closing bites he'd left on her shoulder.

Catalina knew him too well to apologize or ask if he minded. Instead, she said, "I saw a king's armlets in a museum once. They were pure gold. From the size of them, he'd have worn them right there."

"Lucas probably has some of those," Shane said. "But I like yours better. Property of Catalina Mendez."

"All others keep out." She bent to kiss them, her lips hot against his sensitized skin. Then she rested her head on his shoulder, turning deliberately so he could smell her hair.

He never wanted to move from that spot, but he did have one arm free. Without disturbing her, he reached out across the bed to the opposite side from where Catalina kept her flashlight. It was empty, of course, but there was a space where his gun would fit.

"You could keep your gun there, if you like," Catalina said.

Shane was no longer surprised that she'd known what he'd been thinking. After all, he'd known that her flashlight was as much a weapon as a tool.

*Mates know,* he thought.

*Finally,* hissed his panther.

"Want to move in?" Catalina asked, her eyes bright with hope. "I know it's small and the neighborhood's not that great— it was the best I could do on a paramedic's salary— but I like it. But if you hate it, we could both keep our own places. Or I could move in with you, if you really wanted me to and you're okay with the cats moving in too. Your place is probably much nicer."

"Not even close," Shane replied. "Yeah, it's bigger and I'm sure the rent is higher. But I've lived there for a year and it still looks like a hotel room. I've seen barracks with more individual character. Now that I know I'm not going to just vanish some day and never be seen again, I'd like to have a real home. And you've already got one. I'd rather live here, if you want me here."

"Of course I want you here. The kitties will just have to deal."

Shane heard a scratching noise that was almost certainly an annoyed cat, but just maybe could be something more sinister. He moved to get up.

Catalina tightened her arms around him. "Where're you going?"

"To check the front door."

"I locked it," she said. "That's just Natasha trying to get into the cupboard where I keep the catnip. That's locked, too, but she never gives up."

Shane relaxed, trusting her. Her hair fell across his face in tickling strands and smooth locks, soft as cream. He held her tight, utterly content. He didn't need to go anywhere. He had everything he needed, right here.

The soft huff of Catalina's chuckle warmed his cheek. "I can hear you purring."

# A NOTE FROM ZOE CHANT

Thank you for reading *Protector Panther!* I hope you enjoyed it. If you're starting the series here and would like to know more about Shane's team, the first book is *Bodyguard Bear*, the second is *Defender Dragon*, and the fourth is *Warrior Wolf.* All of those books, along with my others, are available at Amazon.com. You can find a complete list of my books at zoechant.com.

If you enjoy *Protection, Inc.*, I highly recommend Lia Silver's *Werewolf Marines (Laura's Wolf, Prisoner,* and *Partner)* and Lauren Esker's *Shifter Agents (Handcuffed to the Bear, Guard Wolf,* and *Dragon's Luck).* All three series have hot romances, exciting action, brave heroines who stand up for their men, hunky heroes who protect their mates with their lives, and teams of shifters who are as close as families. They are all available on Amazon.

The cover of *Protector Panther* was designed by Augusta Scarlett. The kata Shane shows Catalina is called Tomari Bassai, which means "Storming the Fortress.

The Sea of Stars is a real place in the Maldives.

SPECIAL SNEAK PREVIEW

# WARRIOR WOLF

PROTECTION, INC.
# 4

# CHAPTER ONE

## *Raluca*

Raluca fled across the sky on dragonwings, frequently glancing back. It had been an entire day since someone had tried to murder her, but she wasn't taking any chances. She'd given up everything she had in the hope of finally getting to have a life, and she was not going to let some unknown assassin take that from her before she got the chance to experience it.

Her silver wings stretched out wide to catch the sea breeze. Above, the sky was blue as turquoise; below, the ocean was a darker blue, like sapphires.

She possessed both gems in her hoard, along with many others; after she'd renounced her title as crown princess of Viorel, leaped off the palace balcony, and become a dragon in mid-air, she'd flown to her room, transformed into a woman, snatched up the brocade pack that held her hoard, and shifted and flown away again before an alarm could be raised.

Raluca had taken nothing but her hoard and the clothes she'd been wearing, but that had been sufficient. After reluctantly deciding that she could bear to part with a valuable diamond that had been a gift from her evil Uncle Constantine, she'd sold it and had been living off the proceeds ever since. It had been a good choice; that diamond had so many bad associations that she didn't miss it, even though it had sparkled beautifully in the sunlight.

Her uncle had controlled her for her entire life. He'd attempted to force her into a marriage with a man she didn't love to ensure a treaty between their nations that would line his own pockets. He'd even tried to murder her fiancé's true mate! Raluca was well rid of Uncle Constantine and everything that had come from him.

Her thoughts drifted back to that crucial moment when she had declared her independence and fled. She'd felt so free as she'd leapt off the balcony, become a dragon, and soared away. Her entire life had been ruled by her duties as a princess, with Uncle Constantine monitoring and controlling her every action. Now she could do whatever she wanted.

It had taken her less than a week to realize that she had no idea what she wanted.

She'd first met her fiancé, Prince Lucas, when they were both eighteen, awkward teenagers forced into an arranged engagement that neither had the strength of will to refuse. When they'd met again, five years later, both had changed physically. Lucas was taller and broader across the shoulders: a handsome young man, not a boy. Raluca's daily lessons in posture and dance had finally paid off, transforming her from a clumsy girl uncomfortable in her own skin to an elegant dragon princess who controlled every movement of her body with exquisite grace.

But Lucas had changed inside, too. He'd gone to America and become a bodyguard — such a strange job for a prince — and found the courage to defy his family. When he met his mate, the American backpacker with the charming name of Journey, he'd stood up for her, foiled Uncle Constantine's attempt to murder her, and finally given up his kingdom for her. Now Raluca's uncle was in a dungeon for the rest of his life, Lucas was presumably living happily in America with Journey, and Raluca...

Raluca's breath gusted out of her in a dragon-sized sigh, blowing a hole in a cloud. She'd drifted from Venice to Vienna, staying in the best hotels and seeing the famous sights, but none of it had made her happy. She'd thought she'd feel free, but she felt more trapped than ever. With the entire world at her feet, she'd felt lonely and empty.

Until someone broke into her hotel room and tried to stab her to death as she slept.

Some tiny noise must have startled her, for instinct prompted her to roll off the bed before she was even fully awake. She'd fallen to the floor with a thud, opened her eyes, and stared up in shock at a glittering blade poised above her heart. Then the masked assassin holding the knife tried to plunge it home.

But Raluca's dragon speed outmatched the assassin's training. She threw herself to the side. The dagger smashed into the marble floor. Before the man could try again, Raluca transformed. Her unfurling wings flung the black-clad assassin across the room. The flask he'd been holding in his other hand burst against the wall, releasing the distinctive sharp odor of dragonsbane, the poison that prevented dragons from shifting.

The assassin scrambled to his feet and fled out the door. And Raluca, with a distinct feeling of déjà vu, grabbed her hoard pack in her talons and launched off the hotel balcony.

For the first time since her leap from the palace balcony, she felt alive again. The threat to her life jolted her back into the realization of how much she valued it. She might not know *how* she wanted to live, but she definitely *wanted* to live.

Also, she wasn't stupid. That attack hadn't been random— the dragonsbane proved that the assassin knew she was a dragon, and presumably also knew exactly who she was— and Raluca had a good idea of why someone might want her dead. She'd renounced her title, but she had the right to change her mind and reclaim it. As long as she lived, she potentially stood between the throne of Viorel and everyone who was now in line to inherit it.

Unfortunately, that didn't narrow down the suspects as much as one might hope. Raluca had the only clear claim to the throne. With her out of the picture, that left about twenty cousins and other relatives who, last she'd heard, had been fighting over the crown by any means necessary, from duels to debates to very expensive lawsuits. And that wasn't even counting Uncle Constantine, who might have bribed someone from within his cell with the promise of infinite riches once Raluca was dead and he was free.

No matter who was trying to kill her, they'd tracked her down once and could do it again. And they wouldn't give up after one missed chance.

As a dragon, Raluca could defeat a human. But if she was splashed with dragonsbane, she wouldn't be able to transform, and the next assassin would undoubtedly use the dragonsbane first and the knife second. As a human, she had no idea how to fight. Dragon princesses learned feminine arts like embroidery and gem-carving, not sword-fighting or boxing. She needed a bodyguard.

Luckily, she used to be engaged to one.

Raluca didn't know Lucas's home address — they hadn't been in contact since the balcony, and she'd checked into hotels under an assumed name — but his workplace, Protection, Inc., had a website with a business address. And Raluca had looked it up often enough since she'd fled to have it memorized, thinking wistfully of meeting up with the one who would understand why she'd given up her royal title.

She flew over the beaches of Santa Martina, her dragon magic hiding her from sight, and into the city. It wasn't easy finding an address from above, and she had to circle repeatedly before she finally figured out which of the several towering office buildings was the one she was looking for.

Raluca landed on the roof of Protection, Inc. She glanced around to make sure no one was watching, then let her magical invisibility slip away. She thought of human things — the slide of silk between her thighs, the clack of high heels across a marble floor, and the lonely ache in her heart — and became a woman.

To her chagrin, she found herself standing barefoot in a nightgown, wearing no makeup and with her hair rumpled from sleep, clutching a heavy pack. She must look like a hobo! It was hardly the impression she wanted to make, especially if anyone but Lucas, who was as close to a friend as she'd ever had, was at Protection, Inc.

*It could be worse,* Raluca thought. *If I was any other type of shifter, I'd be naked.*

Only dragons could transform and take their clothing and their hoards with them. The reason for that was obvious; Raluca would have fought to the death rather than abandon her hoard. All the same, her lack of nudity was cold comfort. It wasn't even her best nightgown, but a simple fall of pewter silk she'd picked up in Vienna, unadorned and cut low in the chest. Every time she bent over, it threatened to expose her nipples.

Raluca opened her pack, wishing a golden hairbrush and mirror would magically appear. Unfortunately, she knew every item in her hoard by heart, and she had no such things. But she certainly wasn't going to walk into Protection, Inc. half-naked and unadorned. She might have renounced her title, but she wasn't going to disgrace herself.

She combed her hair as best as she could with her fingers and rubbed her eyes, making sure no stray sleep crumbs clung to her lashes. For jewelry, she made do with a pair of pearl hair clips, a delicate silver necklace, a gold and pearl bracelet, and a mere three rings: a band of sapphires, a gold and pearl ring that matched the bracelet, and a ruby ring that had been a favorite since she'd been a little girl.

The touch of gold and gems to her skin gave her confidence and courage. Drawing upon the strength and pride of dragonkind, Raluca strapped on her pack, tugged the nightgown up, lifted her chin, straightened her back, and marched downstairs to knock on the door of Protection, Inc.

A man opened it. He was so huge that he nearly filled the doorway, made of pure muscle without an ounce of fat. His brown hair brushed the top of the doorframe, and his hazel eyes blinked at her in surprise.

"Whoa," said the man in a deep, rumbling voice. "Uh… May I help you?"

Inwardly, Raluca gritted her teeth; outwardly, she drew herself up to her full height. Her nightgown instantly slithered down. She snatched at it and clutched it in her fist, destroying whatever dignity she'd briefly achieved.

"I am looking for Lucas," she said, carefully modulating her voice.

The big man was still staring at her. He probably thought she was a robber bedecked in her ill-gotten finery. "Lucas isn't here. Are you…" He stared some more, his gaze moving from her bare feet to her fistful of silk to her necklace. "…a relative? Or a friend?"

Raluca and Lucas were, in fact, very distantly related, though one had to go back seven generations to find the connection. But she didn't think this strange, large American would care about that.

"I am a friend," Raluca said. "Please give me his home address."

"I'm afraid I can't do that," the man replied. She was both annoyed and impressed at the polite firmness of his tone; Uncle Constantine couldn't have taught him better. "I'm Hal Brennan, and I run Protection, Inc. And you are…?"

He extended his hand just as she swept into a curtsey. Both of them hastily moved to correct their error. Raluca straightened up with a jerk and stuck out her hand, but she was stiff as a robot she'd once seen in a movie. Hal hesitated, then ducked his head and shoulders in a bow that vividly conveyed how embarrassed and awkward he felt to be bowing at all.

In the silence that followed, Raluca looked for a balcony from which to fling herself. Unfortunately, there was none.

Hal's booming laugh shook the walls. "Well, that was a disaster. Let's try again. This time, let's forget about impressing each other. I'm Hal, Lucas's boss. I'm a bear shifter —"

Shocked, Raluca interrupted, "You'd tell me that? You don't even know who I am!"

Hal gestured at her right arm. She'd forgotten that the nightgown, which had straps rather than sleeves, exposed her glittering silver dragonmarks. "Lucas told me what those meant. So I know you're a dragon shifter. Hey, are you his ex-fiancée?"

"We did not complete our engagement ceremony," Raluca began. Then, catching some of Hal's informality, she said, "That is to say, yes. I am Raluca, the princess — former princess — he was to marry."

Hal's grin broadened. "Pleased to meet you! Lucas told us all about you. I wish I could've seen you jump off the balcony. That must've been a sight to see. Why don't you come inside?"

Raluca followed Hal into the lobby. She was immediately struck by one of the framed photos on the wall. It showed the palace of Brandusa at sunset, with a golden dragon soaring overhead. She stepped forward to get a closer look.

"Yeah, that's Lucas," Hal said. "I hope you didn't come to America just to see him. He's on an assignment in another country, deep undercover, and he'll be gone for at least another week. In the meantime, is there anything I can help you with? Maybe find you a hotel?"

If it hadn't been for her years of training, Raluca would have blushed. Forcing back the hot blood that threatened to color her face, she said, "Yes. A hotel recommendation would be greatly appreciated. But also… I need a bodyguard."

"Oh!" Hal's rugged features instantly shifted from amusement to wariness. His body language changed as well, subtly settling into a deceptive relaxation that Raluca knew meant he was ready to fight for his life. She had seen it before, watching the dragon princes train. "Hmm. Well, you're safe for now. No one can break into Protection, Inc. But you can't stay here forever. Could someone have followed you here?"

"Not directly," Raluca said. "I looked behind me as I flew. But I was tracked down once already. And given that Lucas and I parted on good terms, this is a logical place to look for me."

Hal seemed to appreciate her reasoning. "Yeah, you're probably right. Why don't you have a seat? I'll make you some coffee and you can tell me all about it."

Raluca seated herself in an armchair. It gave way pleasantly beneath her, neither too soft nor too hard. The entire office was more comfortable than it looked, warmed to a pleasant temperature rather than air-conditioned to chilliness.

While Hal went into another room, she examined the other photographs on the walls, all of beasts in their natural habitats. (The natural habitat of a dragon, of course, was a palace.) Lucas was the dragon, and Hal had said he was a bear shifter. One photo was of a bear at a river. Perhaps that was Hal in his shifted form. Probably all the bodyguards were shifters, and all the animals in the pictures were them.

Raluca examined them one by one. A tiger stalking through a lush green jungle. A pride of lions lounging on a savannah. A snow leopard leaping across an icy abyss. A panther lying in wait for its prey. A gray wolf with fierce green eyes, leader of a pack. Which would she want to protect her? They all looked equally strong; any of them would be more than a match for a human, or several humans.

Her gaze drifted down the line, then stopped at the wolf. There was something fascinating about him. At first glance, those eyes, deep as emeralds, were filled with ferocity. But as she looked longer, she thought she saw something else beneath the anger, something that echoed in her own heart.

*Loneliness,* hissed her dragon. *Pain.*

*Why would he be lonely?* Raluca silently asked. *He has a pack.*

Her dragon answered with a shrug, a rustle of wings. *I do not know the* why. *I only see what I see.*

Hal returned with a china cup of cappuccino, which he cradled with surprising delicacy in his enormous hands.

"Are those your bodyguards?" Raluca asked, indicating the photos.

Hal nodded, handing her the cup. "Lucas didn't tell you much, did he?"

Raluca's gaze lowered to the coffee. It not only had foam, but a sprinkling of brown powder atop. She wondered if the office had servants, or if Hal had actually made the coffee himself. Perhaps he had, with the aid of a machine. She had seen such things in Europe.

"Our arrangement was a matter of honor, not love," Raluca said. "Lucas told me as much as he felt comfortable revealing in the short time we had together."

She was mildly irritated at the way Hal smiled every time she spoke. His expression was one of amused familiarity, as if she was some relative whom he met only at holidays but whose quirks he found charming rather than annoying. He should not find her familiar. They had only just met.

"You sound just like Lucas when he first came to America," said Hal. "It's really too bad he's not here. Why don't you start at the beginning, and tell me exactly what's going on and why you need a bodyguard? Don't leave anything out — there's details that may not seem important to you, but could mean a lot to me."

Hal sat down behind a desk, and took out a notebook and a pen.

Raluca took a delicate sip of her cappuccino. The powder was chocolate. In her own country of Viorel, it would have been nutmeg. She forced her mind away from how lost and alone and alien she felt, and began, "At the age of eighteen, Lucas and I were promised in marriage…"

She had been trained to recount a tale clearly and with detail; Hal made few interruptions, but took many notes. When she explained her theory that someone wanted her gone to clear their path to the throne, he nodded and said, "That makes sense."

An odd warmth stole into her heart at his simple words. She was used to being respected, of course. But it was for her position and family and wealth, not for her intelligence. She had learned to read people — Uncle Constantine had made her watch him hold diplomatic meetings with politicians or interrogate prisoners, and then quizzed her about them — and so she could see that Hal was used to having to steer clients to the point, and appreciated that he didn't have to do so with her.

"So I need a bodyguard," Raluca concluded. "I do not know how to fight, and I cannot publicly become a dragon. I would die before revealing the existence of shifters to the world. Someone must protect me who can do so in their human form."

Hal nodded; this too made sense to him. "Of course. And I assume you'd like to know who's behind the plot?"

"I would," Raluca said. "So I need someone who is strong, courageous, *and* intelligent."

Hal smiled and leaned back in his own armchair. "That goes without saying. I only hire the sharpest knives in the drawer. But what sort of things do you want to do while they're guarding you? I'd assign a different person depending on whether you want to go to hot new nightclubs, or Santa Martina's fanciest parties." He chuckled, more to himself than to her, as he said, "Or frat keggers and fight clubs and flea markets."

Raluca hadn't had any particular plans other than "find Lucas" and then "get a bodyguard." But Hal's offhand joke struck a chord with her. Why *not* see how the other half lived? She'd had enough fancy parties to last her a lifetime. But she'd never been to a nightclub. She didn't even know what a frat kegger or fight club or flea market was, other than a place or activity Hal wouldn't expect to see her at. Presumably they were rough and low class.

"I want to go to hot new nightclubs," Raluca said. "And also fight clubs and flea markets and — er —" The last term was so unfamiliar to her that it slipped her mind. "That other thing. I want to do everything a princess of Viorel never gets a chance to do. Peasant things. Dangerous things. American things."

Then honesty forced her add, "And also fancy parties. I do enjoy them. I would be very sad to leave America without attending a single ball."

"I think we can get you into at least one." Hal smiled at her. He seemed to sincerely like her, which was pleasant but strange. Most people neither liked nor disliked her; she was the princess, to be regarded with awe and respect and deference. Liking didn't enter into the picture.

"You're in luck," Hal went on. "Almost everyone but Lucas is available right now. Don't get the wrong impression; everyone's extremely competent, and anyone here can protect you. But if it's possible, I try to pick the ideal bodyguard for the job. Would you rather have a man or woman, or does it not matter? Do you want someone who'll look intimidating, or would you rather have someone who people won't even know is your bodyguard?"

Raluca hadn't thought of anything beyond needing *someone* to protect her, since Lucas wasn't there. She had no idea who the other bodyguards were. And though she knew Lucas must trust Hal, or he wouldn't be working for him, she'd been trained her entire life not to reveal anything more than was absolutely necessary.

Cautiously, she said, "Why don't you tell me a little about who you have, and then I'll decide."

To her relief, Hal seemed to find that a reasonable request. "Sure. I'll show you photos, too, so you can get a sense of who might blend in where."

Hal took a file from his desk drawer and opened it. The first photo was of Lucas, looking every inch a dragon prince in a three-piece suit. Hal flipped it over without comment.

The next was of an elegant blonde woman. If Lucas looked like a prince, that woman looked like a young queen. Raluca started to reach out for her, but Hal slid the photo aside.

"Fiona's on an assignment now," he said. "Too bad, I think you'd get along. Maybe you can at least meet her later."

The next picture was of a Latina woman, curvy and small, smiling confidently at the camera. Hal turned that one over as well. "Catalina's a new hire; she's still in training. But you can have your pick of the rest of the team."

"Are you including yourself?" Raluca wouldn't mind having Hal as a bodyguard. He seemed both competent and friendly, and his size alone should intimidate all but the bravest assassins.

"No, sorry," Hal said. "I have my hands full managing the team. I don't usually take solo assignments. But Shane's available. Here."

Hal showed Raluca a photograph of a tall man with black hair and eyes blue as ice. "Shane is a panther shifter, and he has other powers too. He can terrify people by looking into their eyes, and he can also make people not notice him at all. Since it's not clear who's after you or why, someone who can disappear at will might be the best choice.

Shane can not only protect you, he can investigate and infiltrate for you."

Shane wasn't smiling for the camera, and something about him unnerved Raluca. She couldn't imagine enjoying a nightclub — or anything else — with that dark presence at her side.

Politely, she said, "I'd like to see everyone before I choose."

As if Hal had read her mind, he said, "If you'd prefer someone more easygoing, I have two bodyguards who fit that bill."

He spread out two photos. One was of a strikingly handsome Latino man, strong-looking but with a relaxed posture and pleasant expression. The other was of a curvy black woman with lots of braids and a merry smile. She didn't match Raluca's idea of a bodyguard. But both of them did look a lot more friendly than Shane.

"Rafa used to be a Navy SEAL, with me," Hal said. "He's a lion shifter. He can be intimidating if he needs to be, but he won't scare people accidentally. The only problem with him is that if you're hoping to meet men, they may not approach you if they see him with you."

Raluca considered the photo again. "I see what you mean. What about the woman? I assume she's stronger than she looks."

"Absolutely," Hal assured her. "Destiny is a tiger shifter and an Army veteran. She has shifter strength, she's a crack shot, she's very level-headed, and she's equally comfortable on the streets and in high society. Since you don't know who's after you and you want to find out, you're probably better off with a bodyguard who doesn't look like one. Destiny can protect you, but as long as you don't hold hands or anything, anyone who sees you together will assume you're just friends."

Hal gave a firm nod, pushing Destiny's photo closer to Raluca. "Destiny's perfect for you. And you'll get along, I promise."

Destiny did sound good, and Raluca liked the idea of a female bodyguard. She'd had so few opportunities to make friends with other women — or with anyone, for that matter. And while Destiny was casually dressed in the photo, Raluca could also imagine her in an evening gown, perhaps with her hair done up in a more formal style.

Raluca picked up the photo. She was about to say, *"I'll take her,"* when she caught sight of the picture beneath Destiny's.

Curious, Raluca glanced at that one. It showed a young man staring challengingly into the camera, as if he was trying to intimidate the photographer into looking away. His hair was black, his eyes were an unusually intense shade of emerald green, and his muscular arms, which were folded across his chest, were covered in tattoos.

Dragon shifters never tattooed themselves; they were born with dragonmarks, glittering birthmarks the color of their dragon, unique to each individual. Tattooing was a taboo, considered inferior to a dragon shifter's natural marks. Raluca, used to the beauty and elegance of dragonmarks, had always thought that tattoos were tacky at best.

But this man's tattoos were different. Raluca picked up the photograph to get a closer look. Tree branches stretched along his arms, some gnarled and ancient, some young and smooth, with each crack in the bark and vein in the leaves depicted with exquisite detail and realistic shading. A slim vine, green as spring itself, twined around one finger.

The tattoos were cut off by his shirt sleeves, but they obviously extended beyond them. Raluca wondered how much of his body was tattooed. If his arms had branches, would his chest show the trunks? What would the muscles of his chest look like under that exquisite tattoo? Would his nipples be covered in leaves, or left bare? Would wind seem to move in the trees as he breathed in and out…?

A noise made her jerk her gaze upward.

Hal had cleared his throat. "Like I said. Destiny's the one you want. I'll call her right now."

"What about this man?" Raluca held up the photograph.

"Nick?" Hal shook his head. "Not the right guy for this job. I wasn't even going to show him to you."

"Is he not available?"

"Oh, he's available." Hal seemed to be trying not to laugh, as if he had heard the punchline to a joke that Raluca was too ignorant to understand. It annoyed her.

Icily, she inquired, "Is he incompetent? Unintelligent? Weak?"

"No, of course not. He's just — look, you mentioned fancy parties. I assume you mean princess-level fancy parties. That's not Nick's style." Hal chuckled, again seeming amused at some private joke. "He'd be great at the fight clubs, though."

Her dragon hissed within her. *Choose Nick.*

Raluca's dragon was normally very quiet. She'd already spoken more in the last hour than she often did in an entire week. That caught Raluca's attention as much as her words.

Hal reached for the photo.

Instinctively, Raluca jerked it away from him, clutching it to her bosom. "In formal attire, he would wear long sleeves. Most of his tattoos would be covered. If necessary, he could wear gloves to conceal the rest."

It would be a shame to cover up those beautiful tattoos, but those strong hands would also look good in black silk gloves. His big knuckles would make a tempting contrast, a suggestion of roughness beneath the elegance. She could almost imagine the smooth touch of his silk-covered hand on her bare arm as he escorted her to the dance floor. After the dance, when they were alone, she could remove the gloves for him. With her teeth, perhaps. Very delicately, pulling gently, her lips brushing across his muscular wrist and the back of his hand in a trailing kiss, taking her time, making him shudder with pent-up desire…

Hal cleared his throat again. Raluca dropped back to reality with a jolt. What was wrong with her? It was completely unlike her to drift into a sexual fantasy in the middle of a business conversation — especially a fantasy of something so completely inappropriate. She was hiring a guard, not a lover. And if she did take a lover, it would certainly not be a tattoo-covered bodyguard. It would someone suited to her station. If not royalty, at least a man from a high-born family. Or perhaps a billionaire.

Though if she did hire this man — Nick — people might *mistake* him for her lover, as Hal had warned could happen if she was seen with Rafa. The rumor might get back to Viorel. Everyone who had ever known her would be absolutely horrified. Appalled. Disgusted. Furious.

Especially Uncle Constantine. He'd be so enraged to imagine her with this rough, tough, tattooed commoner, he might actually have a stroke.

Raluca smiled. "I choose Nick."

# ZOE CHANT
# COMPLETE BOOK LIST

All books are available through Amazon.com. Check my website, zoechant.com, for my latest releases.

While series should ideally be read in order, all of my books are standalones with happily ever afters and no cliffhangers. This includes books within series.

## BOOKS IN SERIES

***Protection, Inc.***

Book 1: *Bodyguard Bear*
Book 2: *Defender Dragon*
Book 3: *Protector Panther*
Book 4: *Warrior Wolf*

***Bears of Pinerock County***

Book 1: *Sheriff Bear*
Book 2: *Bad Boy Bear*
Book 3: *Alpha Rancher Bear*
Book 4: *Mountain Guardian Bear*

***Cedar Hill Lions***
Book 1: *Lawman Lion*
Book 2: *Guardian Lion*
Book 3: *Rancher Lion*

***Enforcer Bears***
Book 1: *Bear Cop*
Book 2: *Hunter Bear*
Book 3: *Wedding Bear*

***Fire & Rescue Shifters***
Book 1: *Firefighter Dragon*
Book 2: *Firefighter Pegasus*
Book 3: *Firefighter Griffin*

***Glacier Leopards***
Book 1: *The Snow Leopard's Mate*
Book 2: *The Snow Leopard's Baby*

***Gray's Hollow Dragon Shifters***
Book 1: *The Billionaire Dragon Shifter's Mate*
Book 2: *Beauty and the Billionaire Dragon Shifter*
Book 3: *The Billionaire Dragon Shifter's Christmas*
Book 4: *Choosing the Billionaire Dragon Shifters*
Book 5: *The Billionaire Dragon Shifter's Baby*
Book 6: *The Billionaire Dragon Shifter Meets His Match*

***Hollywood Shifters***
Book 1: *Hollywood Bear*
Book 2: *Hollywood Dragon*
Book 3: *Hollywood Tiger*
Book 4: *A Hollywood Shifters' Christmas*

***Honey for the Billionbear***
Book 1: *Honey for the Billionbear*
Book 2: *Guarding His Honey*
Book 3: *The Bear and His Honey*

***Ranch Romeos***
Book 1: *Bear West*
Book 2: *The Billionaire Wolf Needs a Wife*

***Rowland Lions***
Book 1: *Lion's Hunt*
Book 2: *Lion's Mate*

***Shifting Sands Resort***
Book 1: *Tropical Tiger Spy*
Book 2: *Tropical Wounded Wolf*

***Upson Downs***
Book 1: *Target: Billionbear*
Book 2: *A Werewolf's Valentine*

## NON-SERIES BOOKS

## DRAGONS

*The Christmas Dragon's Mate*
*The Dragon Billionaire's Secret Mate*

## EAGLE SHIFTERS

*Wild Flight*

## WOLVES

*Alpha on the Run*
*Healing Her Wolf*
*Undercover Alpha*
*Wolf Home*

## BEARS

*A Pair of Bears*

*Alpha Bear Detective*
*Bear Down*
*Bear Mechanic*
*Bear Watching*
*Bear With Me*
*Bearing Your Soul*
*Bearly There*
*Bought by the Billionbear*
*Country Star Bear*
*Dancing Bearfoot*
*Hero Bear*
*In the Billionbear's Den*
*Kodiak Moment*
*Private Eye Bear's Mate*
*The Bear Comes Home For Christmas*
*The Bear With No Name*
*The Bear's Christmas Bride*
*The Billionbear's Bride*
*The Easter Bunny's Bear*
*The Hawk and Her LumBEARjack*

**BIG CATS**

*Alpha Lion*
*Joining the Jaguar*
*Loved by the Lion*
*Panther's Promise*
*Pursued by the Puma*
*Rescued by the Jaguar*
*Royal Guard Lion*
*The Billionaire Jaguar's Curvy Journalist*
*The Jaguar's Beach Bride*
*The Saber Tooth Tiger's Mate*
*Trusting the Tiger*

**If you love Zoe Chant, you'll also love these books!**

*Laura's Wolf* (*Werewolf Marines # 1),* by Lia Silver. Werewolf Marine Roy Farrell, scarred in body and mind, thinks he has no future. Curvy Laura Kaplan, running from danger and her own guilty secrets, is desperate to escape her past. Together, they have all that they need to heal. A full-length novel.

*Prisoner* (*Werewolf Marines # 2),* by Lia Silver. Werewolf Marine DJ Torres is a born rebel. Genetically engineered assassin Echo was created to be a weapon. When DJ is captured by the agency that made Echo, the two misfits find that they fit together perfectly. A full-length novel.

*Partner (Werewolf Marines # 3),* by Lia Silver. DJ and Echo's relationship grows stronger under fire… until they're confronted by a terrible choice. A full-length novel.

*Mated to the Meerkat,* by Lia Silver. Jasmine Jones, a curvy tabloid reporter, meets her match— in more ways than one— in notorious paparazzi and secret shifter Chance Marcotte. A romantic comedy novelette.

*Handcuffed to the Bear (Shifter Agents # 1)* by Lauren Esker. A bear-shifter ex-mercenary and a curvy lynx shifter searching for her best friend's killer are handcuffed together and hunted in the wilderness. A full-length novel.

*Guard Wolf (Shifter Agents # 2)* by Lauren Esker. Avery is a lone werewolf without a pack; Nicole is a social worker trying to put her life back together. When he shows up with a box of orphaned werewolf puppies, and danger in pursuit, can two lonely people find the family they've been missing in each other? A full-length novel.

*Dragon's Luck (Shifter Agents # 3)* by Lauren Esker. Gecko shifter and infiltration expert Jen Cho teams up with sexy dragon-shifter gambler

"Lucky" Lucado to win a high-stakes poker game. Now they're trapped on a cruise ship full of mobsters, mysterious enemy agents, and evil dragons! A full-length novel.

Manufactured by Amazon.ca
Acheson, AB